CONFESSIONS OF A
FALLING WOMAN

And Other Stories

ALSO BY DEBRA DEAN

The Madonnas of Leningrad

CONFESSIONS OF A FALLING WOMAN

And Other Stories

Debra Dean

HARPER PERENNIAL

NEW YORK ● LONDON ● TORONTO ● SYDNEY

HARPER ● PERENNIAL

Excerpt from "Stopping by Woods on a Snowy Evening" from *The Poetry of Robert Frost* edited by Edward Connery Lathem. Copyright © 1923, 1969 by Henry Holt and Company. Copyright © 1951 by Robert Frost. Reprinted by permission of Henry Holt and Company, LLC.

P.S.™ is a trademark of HarperCollins Publishers.

HarperCollins books may be purchased for educational, business, or sales promotional use. For information please write: Special Markets Department, HarperCollins Publishers, 10 East 53rd Street, New York, NY 10022.

FIRST EDITION

Designed by Justin Dodd

Library of Congress Cataloging-in-Publication Data is available upon request.

ISBN: 978-0-06-082532-4

08 09 10 11 12 ID/RRD 10 9 8 7 6 5 4 3 2 1

Some of these stories have appeared previously in the following magazines and anthologies: "The Afterlife of Lyle Stone" in *Writers' Forum*; "What the Left Hand Is Saying" in *The Seattle Review*; "The Bodhisattva" in *The Bellingham Review* and the anthology *Women's Struggles, Women's Visions*; "The Queen Mother" in *Mid-American Review*; and "Confessions of a Falling Woman" in *Calyx, A Journal of Art and Literature by Women*. My thanks to these publications and their editors.

Thanks, also, to Chang-rae Lee, Ann Reeder, Garrett Hongo, and Tracy Daugherty.

Finally, my deep affection and gratitude to Marly Rusoff and Michael Radulescu, who have blessed me with their nurturing and expertise, and to Claire Wachtel, an editor of sensitivity, humor, and savvy. I'm lucky in you all beyond reason.

To Chip and Kim, Cyn and Dan, and always, Cliff.

CONTENTS

WHAT THE LEFT HAND IS SAYING

Only a mesh of ivy holds this old building upright, ropy veins lashing the fire escape precariously to its side. Wind rattles through the rotting window frames and the tub is in the kitchen, but the building is rent-controlled, so years can go by without a name changing on the buzzers downstairs. Still, before Tim the Puppet Boy arrived, I knew my neighbors in the way New Yorkers do, faces passed on the stairs, voices heard through the walls late at night. In fact, I didn't know a soul in the city. But I'm an only child and the child of only children, and was accustomed to being alone. I wouldn't have called myself lonely.

He arrived in the summer, on a morning already wilting with the heat. I remember I had given up a halfhearted plan to go to a cattle call and instead was soaking in a tub of cold water. He might have been knocking for some time, but

I didn't hear him until I surfaced and reached for another tray of ice cubes out of the freezer. Peering in at the open window was a gangly apparition wearing only striped bikini briefs and ridiculous pink plastic sunglasses. He was sorry to bother me, he said, but could he use my phone?

Oh, for Pete's sake. That was my reaction, can't a person even take a bath in her own kitchen? And then mild astonishment that the fire escape could actually hold the weight of an adult, albeit a pretty scrawny one. A full minute elapsed before it occurred to me to throw a towel over myself. I stood up and tried to shoo him away from the window as though he were a pigeon. He smiled and shrugged but didn't leave.

"I was sunbathing up on the roof, and Juan must have locked the window before he left. Philip's asleep, and it's like trying to wake the dead. You know, you should repot that dracaena—it needs more room for its roots." He was pointing to a dead plant on the sill. "So I've been pounding out there for ten minutes, but no luck." He waited, his smile hopeful.

"Listen, I don't know any Philip or Juan."

"Really?" He seemed disbelieving. "You share a fire escape. I'm staying with them for a few days." He crouched over to extend his hand through the window. "My name's Tim."

I'd never heard of a burglar in a swimsuit, but more to the point, he was the only person I'd ever seen in New York who looked utterly guileless and sexless. I shook his hand and pushed up the sash, cautioning him to watch his step.

Tim stayed for a year. I found out some time later that Philip and Juan had met him only a few weeks before I did. "I thought he was trying to pick me up," Philip said. "Well, my God, he just walked up to me in the park and started talking to me. So I brought him home. Next thing, the little weenie was asleep on the couch."

If I can't remember when Tim moved across the hall into my apartment, it is because he had a disarming lack of boundaries. He'd drop over three times a day—to borrow my iron, to tell me the mail had come, to show me something wonderful he'd found in a Dumpster. In the evenings, he might tap on the door and announce that everyone was watching *Dynasty* on Philip's new TV. Gradually our two doors were simply left ajar. Our two apartments fused, with silverware, shampoo, and condiments migrating freely back and forth. I began to find Tim asleep on my couch when I came home late, and chatting with one of our neighbors in the kitchen when I got up the next morning.

Through Tim, I discovered that our building was populated entirely by aspiring fill-in-the-blanks. I was going to be a star on Broadway or, barring that, sell out and make a lot of money doing television. Juan was a dancer with a company that disbanded and renamed itself every few months, and he hoped to choreograph someday. Philip's aspirations were more vague but nonetheless brilliant: he was going to be famous, for what was left open. Meanwhile, he devoted his energy to being in the right place—whatever club was currently in vogue—and sleeping with the right people. Darla, a would-be model, lived on the second floor. She had once met the photographer Scavullo at a party. He told her she had great bones, and she'd been starving them into prominence ever since, endlessly refining her appearance in hopes of finding the look that would propel her onto the cover of *Vogue*. Her boyfriend, Zak, hung out at the comedy clubs, convinced that he was funny enough to get paid for it. Even Morty the super was taking night classes in real estate. He had big plans to cash in on the co-op boom.

Tim was the only one among us who didn't appear to have any ambitions. He occasionally got work from a company that did rich kids' birthday parties, but there wasn't much demand for puppeteers. He lived more or less hand-to-mouth. The puppets themselves were his own creations, whimsically detailed creatures that he might have sold for a lot of money. More than once I tried to forward this idea, but Tim couldn't sustain any interest in profit. He might spend whole days painting over the same eyes or searching for just the right shade of wool yarn. More often, I heard him playing with an unfinished puppet, cackling laughter and different voices interspersed with his own.

He idolized Jim Henson. Once you knew this about him, it was hard to shake his resemblance to a Muppet. His thin legs and arms moved with floppy abandon, and he tended to dress in childish combinations of color and pattern. But stronger than the physical resemblance, it was the way he moved through the world, as though everyone were his friend. I don't know that he ever actually said so, but I assumed he was from a small town somewhere in the Midwest, a place where people still knew their neighbors and gossiped with them over pie and coffee in each other's kitchens. When he moved in here, the tenants in our building gradually began to mingle and kibitz like a large and affectionate family.

Darla sometimes brought up a six-pack, and Philip would touch up her roots while we drank her beer and listened to her speculate on the infidelities of her boyfriend, Zak.

"He went to the Knicks last night with this bimbo from work, just the two of them. He says, no big deal, she likes the Knicks and she paid for her own ticket, like right, like I'm some kind of moron, so I tell him no woman likes basketball for real. I wasn't accusing him of nothing, just pointing out the obvious, you know?"

Tim nudged me under the table. "You love basketball, don't you."

"For real?" Darla gave me a skeptical look, but you could tell she was hoping it was true.

"Well, I watch it on TV," I lied. "All the time, the Knicks, the Rangers."

Juan rolled his eyes at me behind Darla's back.

That Thanksgiving, it snowed. We had fifteen people for dinner, neighbors and friends and a mail sorter Tim brought home from the deli when Juan sent him out for cranberries. We cooked a twenty-pound turkey in Juan and

Philip's oven, and cornbread and candied yams in ours. Mrs. Zibintzky from downstairs made pumpkin pies, and Morty brought a grocery sack of canned olives and sweet pickles and Cheez Whiz. Zak lugged up a case of beer and bags of ice for the tub, and Darla arranged her mother's china on the two kitchen tables. There wasn't enough room for all of us in any one room, so Tim shuffled food and conversation back and forth across the hall. He was inventing new words to "Over the River and Through the Woods," and every few minutes we got the latest verse, loud and off-key.

"Okay, okay, you guys." Morty stood up and began clanking his fork against a wineglass. "I wanna say a few words on this occasion. I just wanna say that I appreciate you having me into your home. Timmy, I met you, what, two, three months ago and here we are." Morty's eyes welled up. "Eating turkey and so on. Anyways, here's to family, wherever we may find them."

Outside, the lights of the city had receded behind a gauzy curtain of flakes, and the sounds of traffic were muffled and far away. I had the heady sensation that the rooms had somehow come unmoored and we were floating high above the city. Our little group laughed and drank and sang, snug in a cocoon of yellow light, as galaxies of snow whirled past the windows.

Whatever we might later say against him, Tim made us feel like we belonged somewhere.

Zak used to try out his new routines on Tim, who chuckled appreciatively at just about anything. When Zak got on the roster for amateur night at *Catch a Rising Star*, Tim went along as his fan. One night, they came back and announced that Tim had signed up for a slot the following week.

"Oh, for Chrissake, Zak," Darla whispered furiously when Tim left the room. "Like it's not bad enough you have to suffer like that? You have to drag Tim into it? They'll eat him for breakfast. Does he even have any material?"

"He does those jokes with the puppets."

"Oh, sure, yeah right, they're gonna love that. Live at the Tropicana, Shari and Lamb Chop. You are such a dimwit sometimes."

She had a point. Each of us privately imagined Tim, our gentle Tim, being savagely humiliated, thrown to the lions. Still, we all went as a show of support, even Mrs. Zibintzky, who never went anywhere. This is what friends do. The group had once endured four hours of Shakespeare when I played Ophelia at the Little Theatre Under the Bridge. We'd been to a garage in Brooklyn to watch Juan dance with people dressed in Hefty bags. Now, we were going to pay our admissions, buy our watery drinks, and writhe through an evening of bad comedy. Afterward, we intended to lie with enthusiasm and to point out the shortcomings of the audience.

By the time Tim was introduced near the end of the evening, I had downed four or five gin and tonics, which were proving to be less diluted than I'd imagined. The room looked precariously unstable. Through the smoky haze, I watched Tim meander onto the stage and then stand blinking in the glare of the spotlight.

"Hi, my name's Tim." He waited expectantly, with the glazed smile of an actor who has forgotten his next line. The silence stiffened. Finally, Darla sighed and said, "Hi, Tim."

"Well, hi, Darla." He smiled at her gratefully. "That's my friend Darla. Actually, I brought several friends with me tonight." Tim reached into the paper sack at his feet and brought out a skinny puppet with a wide grin. He talked as he fitted the puppet over his hand.

"This nightclub thing is kind of new to me. Usually I do children's parties. You know how kids love puppets. But I think we're all really just kids. My mother thinks so, too. For my birthday, she bought me an extra-large sweater. 'You'll grow into it,' she said."

Our little table responded on cue. We sounded like opera singers laughing, ha ha ha ha.

"Now, this puppet is Rocky. I named him after my mother. I'm just kidding. Actually, Mom's name is Rambo. Rocky, say hi to all the nice folks out there."

The puppet's vacant gaze rested on Tim. "You're dying out here, Tim, you know that?"

"Well, I . . ."

Then the puppet did the bit that's become his trademark. The punchline where he lifts up his hand and all but the middle finger falls over. I still don't think it's funny, but I yelped with laughter at the incongruity of Tim telling a dirty joke. The audience was laughing now, too, and I could feel the tension ease around our table.

Up on the stage, Tim looked genuinely puzzled.

"Please excuse Rocky," Tim said. "I don't know what's gotten into him."

"Your friend Philip, that's what got into me. I'm talking sodomy, Tim. Didn't you notice it's a little sticky in there?" Tim froze, his eyes moving slowly toward his left hand. The room sniggered and squealed.

"Puppet fucker." The puppet leered directly at Philip.

"Rocky, now hush."

"Once you've had a puppet, you never go back. Right, Phil baby?" I looked over at Philip, who smiled good-naturedly at the stage.

Mrs. Zibintzky said, "I may be too old for this."

Tim and Rocky started this riff on plastic surgery. Pretty funny stuff and I was laughing, and then he said something very specific about a neighbor and a botched breast job, and I realized he was talking about Darla. No one was supposed to know. I mean, it was a ridiculous secret, but when you come right down to it, most of our secrets are. I stole a glance at Darla, who was staring rigidly into some middle distance.

"Man, I've got more real parts than she does." The puppet cackled viciously. "It must be hard on that boyfriend of hers."

"Why do you say that?"

"He can't tell for sure when he's two-timing her. 'Did you have your ass done, honey, or am I having another affair?'"

"The little shit," Zak croaked. Darla rose and I started to say something—I don't know what. Zak was already reaching toward her, but her look stopped all of us cold. She left.

My name crackled over the mike.

Tim was looking quizzically at his puppet. "I thought you liked her, Rocky."

"She's a loser, Tim. I went to see her in that Shakespeare play. Man, that was painful."

"Well, it was a tragedy, Rocky."

"You're telling me. She was so bad, the Surgeon General had warnings posted in the program. I ignored that, I'm tough, but Tim, there's a limit to what a human being can endure. Halfway through her mad scene, the audience started chanting 'Jump, Jump, Jump.' First play in New York closed by the Board of Health."

There was more, but the words began to run together, blurring into a howl of laughter. I kept staring at Tim, transfixed by his placid smile. His lips were slightly parted, and I couldn't tell whether they moved when the puppet spoke.

Afterward, we congratulated Tim, not warmly, but he didn't seem to notice. He hugged me and then giddily introduced a man in a slouchy silk suit named Graham. I held out my hand, but Graham had already turned back to Tim.

"Tim, first rule: you don't use real names. You don't want your roommate suing you for libel, now do you?" Graham laughed like someone who gets paid to, which, as it turns out, he does. He works for the cable company where Tim got his first break.

When we left the club, Tim was chatting it up amiably with a bartender and a few others who acted like he was their best and oldest friend. He waved to us happily and said he'd be along later, but he never came back. I heard later he was living in a loft downtown that belongs to some LA muckety-muck.

The apartment building was dark when we returned to it that night, every window a blank. We let ourselves in and I suppose we said good night or something to that effect, but all I recall was the buzzing of the fluorescent tubes in the vestibule and, as I climbed the stairs, the sound of doors shutting quietly below me, one by one, the click of deadbolts turning.

I turn on the television sometimes when I see Tim's name listed in the cable guide. So do Philip and Juan; I can hear the nasty cackle of that puppet on the other side of the wall. The others probably watch him, too, though when I see them on the stairs, we don't mention Tim. We comment on the weather or complain about the boiler going out again. We say we should really get together, but you know how these things go. Time flies.

THE QUEEN MOTHER

When my baby sister called and asked me to fly down from New York, my first thought was that the entire family had finally gone off their rockers.

The idea, as Lizann explained it, was to get the Queen Mother when she was sober and her defenses were down. Everyone would go to a few training sessions beforehand, and then on Saturday meet up at Daddy's office. He'd bring her over there on some pretext and then, well, then I suppose you have to imagine a really horrendous surprise party. Surprise! Your whole family and your best friend are here because we all love you. But (and this is the kicker) this drinking thing is out of hand, and we've made an appointment for you to check in at the local rehab clinic.

"It'd just mean so much to her if you were there, Torrie."

"That's plain craziness. She's hardly going to appreciate my presence at a lynching." I could hear my voice sliding into its old curves, matching the drawl on the other end of the line.

"She'll probably be angry at first." Lizann is truly sweet, so it's hard for her to allow that anyone she loves might behave badly.

"At first? She'll have your butt in a sling for the next ten years." "Well, something's gotta be done before she kills herself. Doctor Jackson tried to talk to her about going to a clinic after she jitterbugged through the French doors at Christmas. He says if she'd been sober she would've broken half the bones in her body. Course, she put on a big show. Told him that she was absolutely horrified at his insinuations, that she never had more than a glass of sherry before dinner. She kept insisting that Tootie had simply put too much wax on the floor before the party. She even tried to fire Tootie." Lizann's laughter tinkled over the wires.

Every family has its stories. In ours, my mother is always the star. She won Miss Baton Rouge 1949 for her rendition of that mockingbird-and-magnolias speech in *Jezebel*, the one where Bette Davis tells Henry Fonda that she's in his blood, "just like the smell of fever mists in the bottoms." Some talent scout met her and invited her out to Hollywood to do a screen test, but as she tells it, she gave all that up to be a wife and a mother. Still, she's never lost her penchant for drama. One year she made us kids dress up in our costumes and dragged us out trick-or-treating on the morning of November first because she'd been too plastered to take us out the night before. At each door, she made a pious little speech about Lizann, her youngest, being sickly, and how she just couldn't let the little ones wander around the neighborhood in the damp of evening. She has an uncanny ability to humiliate, to make you absolutely crazy with rage. Then comes the coy act, or the righteous anger, or her famous imitation of a martyred saint, whatever suits the occasion.

When our brother, Ted, brought Lydia home for the first time, the Queen persisted in calling her Mrs. Gardner. She kept it up all through cocktails and dinner, politely inquiring after the health of Lydia's former in-laws and behaving for all the world as if she didn't know that Lydia had been divorced for almost a year. Afterward, Ted pitched a fit, he really laid into her, but she was too cagey for him.

"Surely your friend doesn't object to good manners." This said with a hand fluttering to her bosom.

"You were deliberately embarrassing her, Mama, with all that talk about her wedding."

"You weren't there, Edward. It was ravishing. Ray Gardner was in the military, you know, so they had that lovely business with the crossed sabers."

"You're a shrew. You knew damn well that she divorced him. You read the notice to me yourself."

"Well, my goodness, darling, I don't commit everything I read in the papers to memory."

It can get funny, so long as you're not on the receiving end. But we all get on her bad side if we cross her.

So I'm still not sure why I promised Lizann I'd take part in this particular drama; I'd worked so hard to get away from them. I went up North for school, a move that was variously interpreted as an insult to the family, to the state of Louisiana, and to Tulane, Daddy's alma mater. When I graduated, I stayed on in Boston and stumbled around for a while, waiting on tables. Every Sunday evening for almost a year, the phone would ring at eight o'clock. I'd grit my teeth like one of Pavlov's dogs hearing a bell, but no matter how hard I tried to match her cordial tone, within ten minutes I'd be screeching into the receiver.

Of course, the last straw was my moving to New York to give the acting thing a go. Actually, her words were "the last nail in my coffin." You might think she'd be pleased that I was so clearly trying to fulfill her fantasy. But there you'd be wrong. She didn't want anyone to upstage her, least of all me. She needn't have worried.

We had a big fight one night that culminated in her telling me that while I had many good qualities, an actress needs a certain sparkle that makes people sit up and take notice. I, in turn, let her know just what I thought of her long-cherished illusion that she herself had this sparkle.

"That so-called studio scout, he wasn't dazzled by your talent, Mama. He wanted to get you in the sack. Jesus, it's the oldest line in the book. 'I could make you a star.' Even I've heard that one, Mama, even dull little me."

Daddy says that they played hide-and-seek with the key to the liquor cabinet for weeks after that phone call. I started spending Christmases and Thanksgivings with friends.

Sometimes guilt did get the better of me, but I always, but always, ended up being sorry. On every plane back to New York, I would swear up and down that this time I had learned my lesson. I guess whoever said that blood is thicker than water knew what they were talking about. I don't know how else to explain going back one more time.

My flight got hung up in Atlanta for hours while they fiddled with a hitch in the landing gear. I sat hunched over the pamphlets Lizann had mailed me, checking my wristwatch and wishing like hell that they'd let us off the plane so I could have a drink and a cigarette. Between booking a last-minute dinner party and my meat supplier losing an order, I'd already missed the first two meetings at Serenity Lane. The way things were going, I might very well miss the final one. Just about the time I'd decided to get off the plane and catch a flight heading back to New York, the pilot's voice crackled over the PA, the lights flickered, and the plane began to lumber forward. It was already dark by the time I landed in New Orleans.

Aunt Maybelle and Uncle Duke were waiting at the airport. Duke grabbed the overnight bag out of my hand as I stepped into the terminal and ushered me through the sparse crowd around the gate to where my aunt sat in the waiting area. He said, "Does this look like our Victoria to you? I'm not at all sure, it's been so long. I just grabbed the prettiest young lady comin' down the ramp."

Maybelle grasped my hand in hers and began to tear up. "Well, we're just so happy to see you, Victoria. We're just so glad. I don't know what in the world—" She broke off, sniffling, and clicked open a patent leather handbag, searching for a hankie. "Your father, poor dear, he'll be so happy. He wanted to come here himself, but he didn't want Ellen to. . . . All this sneakin' around. It makes me feel like a traitor, I swear."

Duke broke in, chuckling. "You still charging them Yankees eighteen dollars for a plate of gumbo and greens?" This is another family joke. I started teaching myself to cook back when I was about thirteen and the Queen took to napping through the late afternoons. By the time she'd come downstairs to collect the sherry that Daddy rationed out to her each evening at cocktail hour, she'd already be too stupefied to put together a meal. I never was a fancy cook, but I loved tying an apron around my waist and feeding people. The catering business started out as a sideline, something to tide me over between acting jobs, but when the Cajun rage hit New York, I became sort of a small-time Colonel Sanders. I provide the local color, a trumped-up version of Southern hospitality, and my Grandmother Wilene's recipes for cornbread and bourbon pie.

The meeting at the clinic had already started by the time we arrived. Ted was in the middle of reciting something, but when the three of us slipped in he stammered to a halt. A dumpling-faced man with blond wisps of hair combed across his scalp smiled and waved us into empty chairs near the door. Everyone else in the room I knew: Daddy, Lydia, Lizann, and my mother's friend, Winnie.

"Ted, that was just fine. We'll pick this up again in a minute, after we get Torrie here oriented a little. Torrie" —the man shifted his smile to me—"my name is Henry Bujone, and I'm going to be assisting in this intervention. I understand that you had a difficult time getting down here. But you're here now, and that's going to mean so much to your loved one." Henry's voice rolled like molasses, the long steady drawl of a preacher. "Lizann here tells me you used to be an actress. Might I have seen you in anything?"

"You might have." I left it at that. I don't know why, but I took an instant dislike to the man.

"Well, then." He cleared his throat and resumed, "We're just doing a little role-playing here. Kind of like a rehearsal for what we're gonna say tomorrow. Everyone here has made a list of specific events and times when the dependent's drinking has impacted on their lives. Did you get a chance to read the literature?"

I nodded, trying hard to keep my own smile from cracking into a smirk. No one who'd met the Queen Mother even once would call her dependent. Imperious, manipulative, and phony, yes, but not dependent.

"Well, if you have any questions, you feel free to speak right up. Let's see, Ted, you were telling your mother about the time she dropped your little boy. Why don't you tell her how that made you feel?"

Ted scrutinized the sheet of yellow legal paper in his lap.

"It made me scared and, well, kinda angry. I know she didn't mean to, but . . ."

"Tell it to her, Ted."

My brother cleared his throat and turned to Winnie. She, in turn, pursed her lips and glared at him, in a passable imitation of the Queen. What followed resembled the worst of the soaps: bad actors sitting around on a living room set and rehashing family traumas. You know, like "Tiffany, how could you leave Rock lying in that hospital bed dying of cancer, and run off to Monte Carlo with his best friend, Stone?" I sat there like a housewife riveted to the tube, worse really, since I already knew most of the plot turns. The Queen Mother would smash up the Lincoln in the parking lot of the Piggly Wiggly and then throw a hissy fit because her husband wouldn't sue the guy she'd backed into. Lizann would be too embarrassed to bring her friends home because one time they'd found her mother passed out on the front lawn, and she'd had to lie and say the Queen was sunbathing.

I sat watching in fascinated horror as my entire family aired their dirty laundry in front of Henry, weeping and telling Winnie, Queen for a day, how much they loved her, how concerned they were for her welfare.

Daddy was the hardest to watch, though. When his turn came, his voice was so low and gravelly I could hardly make out the words. He told Winnie that he would love her till the day he died, but that he had packed two suitcases, one for each of them, and that if she didn't use hers, he would take his and go home with his son. A few tears pooled in the leathery folds under his eyes. Daddy hadn't cried since they shot Jack Kennedy in Dallas. He'd always been a proud man.

"Torrie, is there anything you'd like to say to your mother? I know you don't have your list made up yet, but if there's some particular incident that comes to mind, you might want to have a trial run tonight."

I wanted to choke the little weasel. I wanted to go home.

"I think I'd rather wait, but thank you, Mr. Bujone." I gave him my best beauty pageant smile.

I sat up half that night in Ted's study, trying to finish the list ol' Henry outlined for me after the meeting.

"First, we need to just shower her with love," he had said. "The alcoholic is so guilty, they think no one could possibly love them. She needs to hear that y'all are here because you care for her. Just write whatever is in your heart. The rest I call data. Choose a few incidents when her drinking has affected you. Specific times and dates, if you can remember them."

The data part was fairly easy, once I got past the idea that I was actually supposed to say everything I was writing.

Once I got past that, I swear it was like a dam burst. That's the wonderful thing about writing, I suppose: there's no one there to talk back to you.

I hunched over the little desk in the corner of Ted's pine-paneled study, filling up page after page with bad memories. I heard Lydia go upstairs, and later Ted stopped at the door to tell me that they'd made up the bed in the guest room and the pink towels in the bathroom were for me. I blew him a kiss and turned back to my list of the Queen's transgressions. All the mornings that she was too hungover to get out of bed, and I fixed Lizann her lunches and dressed her for school. The times she borrowed my allowance for booze or made me tell Daddy that I needed five dollars for a movie ticket. I could write a book on the Queen Mother. Damn near did.

The opening part was what hung me up. It had been easily twenty years since I'd told the Queen I loved her. It never came up. Even the words on paper looked unconvincing. I stayed up until three in the morning, writing "I love you, Mother" and reading it back, crumpling up the paper and starting over, trying to find words that didn't sound phony when I said them out loud. I turned off the desk lamp and carried my pad and pen over to the sofa. I sat in the dark, watching the moonlight fall in opal slats through the venetian blinds, and rehearsed my greeting card sentiments.

Early the next morning, Lydia was tapping on the door of the study. I'd spent a wretched night on the sofa and felt as shaky and surly as if I had a hangover. This was decidedly not the case—Ted and Lydia didn't keep a drop in the house, not even for guests. Lydia stuck her head into the room and apologized for waking me, but we had to leave in an hour. Muffins and coffee were out in the breakfast room whenever I was ready.

I pulled myself up on the sofa and flicked on the end table lamp. A pool of light fell on the pad of lined paper. Except for a few crossed-out lines, the top sheet was blank. To hell with her, I thought. Why else would I be here if I didn't love her?

Daddy's law office is on the fifth floor of the old Mercantile Building downtown. I don't think he has more than five or ten clients nowadays, but he goes down to the office every weekday, dressed in his gray worsted suit, French cuffs, and bow tie. He used to talk about retiring to the Gulf Coast, but he never has, nor do I imagine he will if he can help it. He needs the hours away from her, a little peace between the storms.

Lizann and Henry had dragged extra chairs from the secretary's room next door and hauled the old leather chesterfield back against the wooden file cabinets to make room. The windows behind Daddy's desk were steamed over and streaked with rain, and the room was heavy with that cottony silence peculiar to office buildings on the weekend. As each person filed in, Winnie and then Duke and Maybelle, there was a brief spasm of chatter and then a sinking quiet.

I chose a chair wedged between the desk and a glass-fronted bookcase, and pretended to study the cracked leather spines of old law books and the parchment diplomas on the wall. On Daddy's desk was a silver framed portrait. It was of the Queen Mother on their wedding day, an enormous floral bouquet obscuring her gown, and the thick folds of a satin train arranged in a fan around her ankles. She stood erect and gazed solemnly past the photographer, in the formal style of the day. I remembered this photograph from my childhood; it had seemed to me the absolute height of elegance. Our mother frequently told us that she had named her children after royalty: Victoria, Edward, and Elizabeth. I had come up with the confused notion that my name ensured I would grow up to be as magnificent as the woman in the photograph. But then, I'd been a foolish, dreamy child: I had also believed in Santa Claus until well past my eighth birthday.

Down the hall, the elevator bell rang. Eight pairs of eyes riveted on the door. The window air conditioner coughed and rattled away, the only noise in the room. I strained to hear the clicking of the Queen's pumps, the false pitch of Daddy's voice as they approached. The thick, chicoried coffee I'd drunk for breakfast lurched through my blood, pinging like electricity in my stomach. I wanted to crawl under the desk.

The woman who came through that door was no longer magnificent. In the six years since I'd last seen her, she seemed to have visibly shrunk. Except for her pouching belly, all the flesh had withered off her, and she looked as scrawny and pitiful as a newborn chicken. Clearly, she had believed this to be a special occasion of some sort: she had worn a ruffled organdy dress, and her pinkish hair was tortured into vapory little puffs above her scalp, the work of some demon hairdresser.

There was a moment then, just a second, when I couldn't believe that this woman had ever tyrannized me, that I had ever thought my life depended on getting away from her. She seemed too fragile and pathetic to hurt a fly.

She froze just inside the door, her vague eyes sharpening with horror, and then she composed a wary smile.

"What, in the name of heaven, is going on here? Thomas, I believe you have some explaining to do." Her eyes flitted to Henry, and then to me, and she edged back a step.

"Are we *all* going to Biloxi?"

Henry rose from his chair, introduced himself, and explained that he was a counselor who'd been called in by her family. Her family had some things they wanted to say to her, and he wanted her promise that she would listen to us all before she responded. Her smile fell away and she lifted her chin, staring at some point above his head.

"Anything my family has to say to me, they could certainly say without calling a meeting." Her voice wavered.

"I'd like you to promise to listen to them."

There was a long silence.

"Why, of course." She lowered herself into the chair that Daddy held for her, holding her eyes to that same invisible spot.

I only remember snatches of what was said, but it was excruciating to watch. When I was a child, Tootie once took me to a revival meeting at the state fairgrounds. It was truly a terrifying experience, waves of people springing to their feet and singing out feverish confessions, weeping and wailing like a pack of lunatics. I remember feeling like I was being drowned, my lungs filling up with other people's tears.

My family are lapsed Episcopalians and not practiced in such ritual displays of emotion, but for amateurs, they put on quite a show. Lizann stumbled over her lines; Maybelle cried in jagged fits and starts; Duke squirmed and twitched like a dog plagued with fleas. Daddy, looking like a man sentenced to die, paced a slow circle behind his wife, plucking at his chin and wiping his eyes.

Throughout, the Queen Mother perched rigidly in her chair and stared off into space, not betraying for a minute that she was aware of the bedlam surrounding her. It was unnerving, as I'm sure she intended it to be. Excepting an occasional flinch, she held herself as still and dignified as the portrait on Daddy's desk.

When my turn came around, I stared at the pad in my hands, covered with the angry words of the previous night. She'd heard it all before, every last sniveling complaint. I wondered how, after all these years, we had thought that a confrontation was going to get us anywhere. One more go around the block wasn't going to make a difference.

"Mama, I think I'm going to just pass." In the corner of my eye, I saw Henry lean forward apprehensively. Passing was obviously against the rules; we weren't playing bridge. I turned back to the Queen and pushed on.

"I don't even know why I came down here. I really don't have anything left to say. I thought I did, but I don't. If you decide to stop drinking, fine. But it's your own life, and I'm tired of messing in it." I could hear the water rising over my voice. "I was tired of it years ago, Mama."

The Queen Mother continued to gaze impassively at the window.

When Daddy had said his piece, Henry quietly explained to the Queen that there was a bed open for her at Serenity Lane and that, with her permission, the family would drive her over there. He asked her if she had anything to say.

The room fell silent. We all waited on her. I guess everyone was still hoping she would give herself up, break down in sobs of relief or repentance or whatever. But when she did speak, her voice all cool and satiny, we came to our senses quick enough.

She rose to her feet and fastened her eyes on Henry.

"I can just imagine how difficult this must be for you, Mr. Bujone. I have always wondered how those psychiatrists did it. Day in, day out, mucking around in the private lives of complete strangers. Myself, I would simply die of shame.

I hope your superiors will not regard this as a failing on your part. I would be happy to write a note expressing my sincere admiration of your abilities. Victoria, would you be so kind as to drive me home now?"

With that, she nodded shortly to me and walked out of the room. We remained behind, slumped in our chairs like a bunch of balloons with the air let out. Henry Bujone, unwilling to admit defeat, launched into his stock of dim-witted platitudes, reminding us that we each had personal victories to take home with us that day. Some people should just be taken out and shot.

When I came out to the parking lot, I saw her sitting in the backseat of Daddy's Lincoln. I slipped into the driver's seat and gripped the wheel to steady the tremor in my hands. If I had been wondering why I was selected to chauffeur, she solved the mystery for me.

"I'll thank you to remember that you have nothing more to say to me."

We drove silently through town, until I started to turn onto Hundred Oaks Avenue.

"No, stay on the Acadian until Broussard." It had been years since I'd lived there, but I still knew the way home. I glanced in the rearview mirror and saw the Queen sunk low into the plush velour seat, staring out the side window. I drove on, the windshield wipers clicking away the drizzle. When we got to Broussard, she commanded a left turn and then, just before City Park, "On the right here, please, Victoria."

It was the clinic I had been to the previous night. In the daylight, it looked shabbier: a sagging old Victorian house with a newer two-story wing grafted awkwardly onto its side. There were no identifying signs, just the red paint at the curb that spelled out Emergency Vehicles Only.

I shut off the engine and raised my eyes to the rearview mirror. Her powdered face was streaked with tears. When I turned around, her eyes met mine for the first time that day, really for the first time I can remember.

"You may tell everyone I have decided I need a rest. Your father and I were planning a week in Biloxi, but tell him I've changed my mind. It's become such a touristy place, and I really feel I need some peace and quiet."

There wasn't a quieter place on the planet than the inside of that car. Peace is harder to come by.

"Mama," I said. "I love you." Just like that, like exhaling after too long a time underwater. And then it was quiet again. I listened to the clock on the dashboard ticking away, the sound of tires swishing by on the wet pavement. My eyes followed a drop of rain as it slid slowly down the length of the windshield, welding to another drop and then sliding again.

THE AFTERLIFE OF LYLE STONE

Lyle had been going to the records storage room and somehow had gotten lost, taken a wrong turn somewhere and was wandering down long gray-carpeted hallways with no doors. Music pulsed through the walls, an interminable cello rendition of "I Heard It Through the Grapevine"; the fluorescent lights overhead buzzed a backbeat. He turned down one passageway after another, thinking eventually he would find a door or a familiar landmark or a person who could direct him back to the offices of Stickel, Porter, Rathburn & Webb. Then at the end of a particularly long corridor, there loomed a door, heavy double doors actually, with a brass plaque that said Conference Room J. He poked his head into the room and saw maybe a dozen people seated around an enormous mahogany conference table. Apparently he had interrupted a meeting, for the conversation ceased and all heads turned toward him. He was about to apologize when he recognized the faces: Chad Rathburn and two of the attorneys from Estate Planning, and his wife, Jen, was there also, looking very cool and pretty in a pink wool suit. Next to her, Dave Whitsop, Lyle's biology class partner in the ninth grade, squeezed Jen's arm and leaned in to mouth something in her ear. Around the far end of the table, he saw his friend Bill, a woman he had dated briefly in college, and his father, which was puzzling because the latter had been dead for eight years. He started to say something, but his father pursed his lips and shook his head almost imperceptibly, and suddenly it occurred to Lyle that he had done something wrong.

"Lyle"—Chad Rathburn broke the silence—"come in."

There were no empty chairs around the table so Lyle shut the door behind him and remained standing obediently just inside it.

"We'd hoped to give you an opportunity to explain your-self, but frankly"—here Chad glanced meaningfully at his watch—"frankly, we've already wasted a lot of time here and I've got a three o'clock. And I think your actions pretty much speak for themselves."

"Actions?"

"Well, not to put too fine a point on it, it's certainly not the kind of performance we expect."

"I, I don't understand." Lyle felt panic like heat rash prickling over his body; he couldn't remember preparing for this meeting.

"Okay, I won't mince words. After giving a good deal of consideration to the question of your future, and I think I speak for everyone here"—Chad slicked a palm over his balding skull—"there's not much evidence."

The room rippled and swelled as though underwater. Lyle's eyes darted around the table; the faces, lit from beneath by small banker's lamps, glared back green and implacable. He noticed his daughter, still five or six years old, doodling on the legal pad in front of her.

"You're going to kill me, aren't you?" The question popped out of his mouth as unexpectedly as a goldfish.

"That boat's already sailed, Lyle. I thought you grasped at least that much." Eyebrows lifted in amusement, and Dave Whitsop smirked and muttered something about the pope's being a Catholic.

"Pay attention, son," Lyle's father ordered.

"Actually, I think that about wraps it up." Chad began gathering together a sheaf of papers spread out in front of him. "You can leave that way, Lyle." He nodded toward a glass wall at the far end of the conference room. Lyle could see, through the panes, a bruised gray sky—no other buildings, nothing at all. He felt himself sliding involuntarily toward the window and when he peered out, he saw that the building was suspended in a roiling fog. He turned to Jen and pleaded with her; get me out of here, he heard his voice saying, but she returned his gaze impassively.

"Don't be dramatic, Lyle. Just go to hell."

Lyle was falling, a horrible blind free fall that turned his insides to water. Toppling backward, he flung out his arms like broken wings, desperately clawing at the rush of space, and he felt the sickening sensation of air moving right through them. He plunged down and down, endlessly through the void, his body and mind displaced by gaseous terror. At the outer fringes of his reeling, he heard a sound. It was the screeching alarm of crows. *Caw, caw, caw.* And then his eyes jerked open and he recognized the sound as his own strangled whimpers.

He was in hell. He was sure of that much, though he couldn't see into the blackness. Something was wrapped around his torso like a winding sheet, preventing him from moving his limbs. He listened to his heart stutter frantically and replayed the horror of falling. Slowly, as his eyes adjusted to the dark, he noticed blood-red numbers blinking slowly out of the black: 4:08, they read. Trembling, he reached into the darkness toward the spot above the numbers where the light switch in his bedroom had been.

What appeared resembled in its spareness the bedroom Jen had had redecorated five years ago. He was lying on a bed raised just a few inches above the bare floor, and he was twisted up in a white comforter. Other than the bed, there were few landmarks in the room for Lyle to seize on. "I see this room very Zen," the decorator had crooned, before removing every throw pillow, every scrap of chintz and bit of color, even the framed photographs of their two children. The only purely decorative object that she'd allowed, an amorphous chunk of granite, was perched on a stand and lit with a halogen spot. Lyle recalled how he had been cowed into approval by the enormous price tag.

He glanced again at the clock: 4:10. Time didn't pass in eternity, did it? Still, he couldn't shake the sensation of being outside his body, a chill awareness as though his eyes were video cameras. Though he recognized every surface and object in the room, they were drained of the pulse of the familiar. He had the disturbing suspicion that if he were to step through the bedroom door, it would open back onto the nightmarish maze of corridors. That was what felt real: the looming conference room doors that had evaporated once he was inside, acne-blotched Dave Whitsop snickering at his discomfort, his wife's placid composure when she told him to go to hell.

Lyle remained motionless in bed and watched the sluggish advance of minutes until the clock read 6:00. Then he disentangled himself from the bedding and forced himself to his feet, mimicking as best he could his usual morning routine. Brush teeth, shower, shave, select a suit and shirt from the closet. Each closet and drawer that he opened contained exactly what it should have, though this did not soothe him. The reflection in the mirror when he shaved looked like the face of someone he knew but couldn't quite put with a name. And when the door opened and Jen glided into the room, a strange voice leaped out of his throat, squeaking with hysteria.

"Where were you? You were gone. I thought you were gone."

Jen glanced at him, her eyebrows arched. "I slept in the guest room. You know, if you could hear yourself snore, you'd do something about it." He reached out to touch her, but she was disappearing into the bathroom.

"I had a nightmare," he said, but there was only the hollow thrumming of the shower.

He couldn't shake it. Lyle moved through the days and then weeks, enveloped in his nightmare. Driving to work on that first morning, he noted that the river of red lights snaking toward downtown Seattle in the predawn looked evil, like brimstone, and the air venting into his car smelled distinctly of sulfur. By the time he arrived at the glass monolith where his office was located and circled, level by level, into the concrete bowels of its parking garage, dampness was trickling from under his arms and down his ribs. He sat in his assigned space on Level 6 for nearly ten minutes, gripping the sweaty wheel and repeating like a mantra, "wake up and get ahold of yourself" before he was able to will himself out of the car, up the elevator, and through the reception area of Stickel, Porter, Rathburn & Webb. After that, he stopped parking underground and found a lot five blocks away.

Slumped in his leather office chair, he would stare out the window at the skyline, shrouded in the perpetual drizzle of February. Occasionally, he would swivel around to again scrutinize the paper on his desk, but everything seemed to be written in code: ". . . except as provided in subsection (c) of this section, the trustee may avoid any transfer of an interest of the debtor in property to or for the benefit of a creditor, for or on account of an antecedent debt owed by the debtor before such transfer was made. . . ." Somehow he would manage to decipher some of the scrit and even to construct a few similarly unintelligible sentences. Every hour or so, he would summon the courage to pick up the phone and return a call. Bewildered by the garbled rattle of voices on the other end, he could only guess at meanings and wondered if any-one noticed the strangled confusion of his replies. He would exhaust himself with these efforts and then, like Sisyphus, return the next morning to discover a fresh drift of pink message slips and another neat stack of documents.

He was terrified to sleep, though after a few nights he hardly knew whether he drifted on one side or the other of consciousness. Even during the day, images from his night-mare rose up unbidden: the walls of Conference Room J wavering in the dim green light; Bill winking lewdly at his daughter and making paper airplanes that skittered to life across the surface of the table like insects; the grim set of his father's jaw as he turned away from Lyle, refusing to answer when Lyle begged him to say what he had done wrong.

His father, while he was alive, had indeed been a taciturn man, a trait Lyle realized he had probably inherited. But he was fairly certain his father would approve of the life he had made. Partner in a blue-chip firm, two kids tucked away in private colleges, a three-car garage stocked with German-made autos—Lyle could tick off a long list of possessions and accomplishments. Membership at Overlake Golf and Country. A Patek Philippe chronograph with the gold strap. The body fat ratio of a twenty-nine-year-old. Lyle stared out the window of his office, watching a gull wheel and scream through the dishwater sky. He tried to recall if he had once felt pleasure in any of it.

He was escaping to the elevator one evening. The buzz of approaching helicopters was at his back and when he turned, Chad Rathburn's face swam into view, magnified as though through aquarium glass. "Just the man I'm looking for," Lyle heard, before Chad's words dissolved again into a thwapping drone. Lyle cowered in mute terror, watching Chad's lips move and nodding repeatedly to mime compre-hension. He waited to see if Chad's expression would darken into disapproval. After a gluey stretch of minutes, though, Chad merely clapped him on the back, a sadistic grin peeling open his face, and, turning on his heel, barked gleefully back down the hall. Perhaps, Lyle thought, no one noticed the change in him because there was nothing to notice. He tried to remember if his life had been different before.

He wanted to tell Jen about the nightmare, about his fears that he was a dead man, but after that first morning when he had blurted out his terror, he could never find an appropriate moment to bring it up. Often, he would arrive home to find an aluminum tray of Guiltless Gourmet sweating on the kitchen counter, next to a note reminding him of her book club or an appointment with the massage therapist. Weekends were penciled solid with charity auctions or small get-togethers celebrating the birthdays and anniversaries of friends or one of the kids home from school. But even when they were alone together, he found it difficult to straddle the years of their habitual exchanges and confess to something so hugely awkward. One night while they were sitting in front of the television, he made an attempt. They were watching what Lyle supposed must be a situation comedy because at regular intervals the vapid chatter was interrupted by bursts of staccato laughter. The hollowness of the laughter chilled him, and he imagined an invisible throng of the damned guffawing and chuckling on cue. He glanced over at Jen and said, "Do you ever wonder if maybe everyone else is just pretending to have a good time?"

"Hmm?" Jen was scratching items onto and off a list in her lap.

"Are you happy, Jen?"

"Of course," she answered absently. Then her pen paused over the list and she raised her eyes over the rims of her reading glasses. Lyle thought he saw a glint of apprehension.

"Why?"

"Maybe it's nothing. I just haven't been feeling like my old self. I can hardly drag myself through the day. I had this nightmare, Jen. I was in hell. . . ." He lapsed into silence, exhausted by the effort of wrenching out so many words.

Jen's features relaxed into mild solicitude. "Maybe you should get Dr. Fiedler to give you something to help you sleep. If you're not getting your rest, that can color your whole outlook."

Usually Lyle had the deli downstairs send up a club on dry toast, but one afternoon he told himself that what he needed was some fresh air. Shuffling through the chill drizzle, his steps turned down the hill toward the waterfront. He found himself at a tiny park, really just a square of pavement wedged between the piers, with two benches occupied by sleeping winos and a bronze plaque commemorating some founding fathers. Lyle stood at the iron railing and looked out at the bay and the sky, a single gray curtain of water. Already, the afternoon was so dim that the ferries lumbering in and out of the mist were lit up and glowing. As a boy, Lyle had aspired to become a ship's captain, but his knee-buckling seasickness had put the kibosh on that idea. It had never occurred to him until just this moment that he might have worked the ferries trolling the calm inland waters of Puget Sound. He wondered if it was too late for such a thing, maybe not captaining, but working the decks perhaps. He could imagine himself dressed in a heavy work vest and boots, waving cars onto the deck and shoving wooden blocks under their front tires, casting the thick lines ashore, sipping on a cup of scalding coffee and whistling as he watched the skyline pull away behind him. He could also imagine Jen's consternation and the ridicule of everyone he knew.

But he might board a ferry anyway, if only as a passenger. Head across the water to the Olympic Mountains on the far side. It would be peaceful to go to sleep on one of those shrouded peaks, to freeze to death in a pillow of snow. He might take a ferry out to the peninsula, drive until he found a mountain, and then hike the rest of the way in. But he felt too lethargic to make the effort. He looked down at the oily slick of water beyond the railing, the paper cups and brown froth that slopped against the pilings, and briefly considered hoisting himself over the side. Even if he succeeded in killing himself, though (and this seemed unlikely given that the surface was only a few feet below and he was a strong swimmer), he greatly feared that it wouldn't end his torment. After all, he was already dead. "That boat's already sailed, Lyle. I thought you grasped at least that much." Turning from the water, he trudged uphill toward the office. A ferry horn bellowed mournfully, sadder than a train's whistle.

When Jen got home from her Jazzercise class, there was a message from Chad Rathburn on the answering machine. Lyle had been found curled in a ball on the floor of the men's room, sobbing incoherently. An appointment was made with Marv Fiedler who, after a brief consultation, prescribed Prozac and also advised Lyle to take some serious R and R:

a little sunshine might help put things in perspective. Lyle and Jen booked two weeks at the Ka'anapali Hyatt, and every morning Lyle washed a pill down with guava juice, donned colorful slacks and a polo shirt, and wound his way around the course, dutifully whacking a ball through nine holes. Slowly, as if coming out of a dream, he began to enjoy himself, and by the time he returned to Seattle, sunburned and laden with pineapples, the whole episode seemed mildly ridiculous and embarrassing.

He tried to pass off his collapse in the men's room as a bout with the flu, but word had already leaked out. Colleagues and acquaintances were suddenly and distastefully intimate, an astonishing number pulling him aside and confessing that they too were on antidepressants and it was nothing to be ashamed of. Merely a chemical imbalance. Hey, the stuff doesn't even give you a good high, they would joke. Any sizable gathering would produce at least one more person who felt compelled to relate his personal journey through the slough of despond or to itemize the contents of her medicine cabinet. "I wasted months in therapy talking about my dreams," one young paralegal confided. "Frankly, I don't have the time for all that navel-gazing. I'm just so much more productive now."

Apparently, he had passed through some contemporary rite of passage and now had to endure the attentions due an initiate. Even those of the evangelistic receptionist who pressed a Post-it note into his hand with the name of a book that had changed her life. He wanted to protest the presumption that his life needed changing, but instead he nodded and thanked her, doing his best to conceal his impatience. Of course, he should expect some uncomfortable jogs before his days settled into the old grooves, but he looked forward to the time when he could finally put this whole business behind him and get on with the rest of his life.

A BRIEF HISTORY OF US

We are all chameleons in my family, always adaptive, always reflecting back whatever environment we're in. Of indeterminate Anglo ancestry, we're mutts, with not even the identifying marks of a Scot's plaid or a German weakness for bratwurst. Our religion mutates safely among interchangeable Protestant sects. Our history tells a story, though not, strictly speaking, our own.

Look back two hundred years and you will find us somewhere in the picture, blending into the scenery. Our ancestors fought in the American Revolution and the Civil War, always on the winning side. We still have great-uncle Howard's sword. Then we moved west with the railroads. There are photographs of us dressed in coveralls and straw hats, sowing wheat across the plains of Kansas. We are posed in front of tepees in North Dakota, the small children in starched petticoats standing next to a Sioux chief. During World War II, we worked in the shipyards and manned the lookout towers, and after V-J Day we all moved to the suburbs.

My own small part in our history began in 1957. I was the first child of a young couple who bore a striking resemblance to Jack and Jackie. She was slender and quiet, always poised in her matching heels and pillbox hat. He was a go-getter, as handsome as a quarterback, smiling into his future. Their pictures appeared in the local newspapers above articles about the Chamber of Commerce and the Junior League's spring fashion show.

I was supposed to be a boy, but since I was not, they changed my name and had another child fifteen months later, also a girl, and then there was a miscarriage that we don't talk about.

Here is a color Polaroid of us. My mother, my sister, and I are all dressed alike because we are girls and it is Easter Sunday and our mother has made us each outfits. Because it is the late sixties, the fabric is a bright, flowery cotton brought back from a Hawaiian vacation. We stand in a row, each of us clutching our purses with cotton gloves. My sister is the one who will not smile for the camera. This is the only clue that we are not entirely as we would like to appear.

A few years later, my mother begins to resemble Mary Tyler Moore, and my father grows a mustache in imitation of Robert Redford. Our pigment darkens into burnished tans. Predictably, we have taken up skiing. Après-ski, we drink Chablis and eat quiche in the lodge. This was taken in Aspen or Sun Valley. My close-lipped smile hides a tangle of braces.

I am by now in the flux of adolescence and perfecting my genetic mutability, an honor student who hangs out with unsavory types in parking lots. I sing in the youth group choir on Sunday mornings, still hung over from the night before. I have come to realize, without being told, that my survival depends on being all things to all people, so I lie about my age and my whereabouts and my friends. My sister, less agile, gets caught smoking dope and is suspended from school.

It is nearing the eighties: my father drives a Mercedes, my mother starts up an interior design business, and my sister gets pregnant and keeps the baby. I graduate from a small liberal arts college, with a double major in drama and poli sci. We haven't seen each other for weeks, but we leave messages next to the phone. When my father meets the younger woman, we get divorced like everyone else. Even our few tragedies feel impersonal, borrowed.

I move to New York to become an actress. What better use of my inherited talents than this? I mouth other people's words with agility, I can simulate anger and joy and horror. I am as comfortable on stage as in my own living room, more so actually. When I go to auditions, the long line of my family trails invisibly behind me. They're a little nervous. They've never had an actor in the family, though come to think of it, someone on the paternal side was in a silent film once. While I'm belting a show tune, I hear them whisper in my ear. They tell me I'm a little flat. I blow the audition, but they say they're proud of me. No matter what I do. They ask me if I've met anyone famous yet. They wonder when I'm going to be on *The Tonight Show*.

When I join the Screen Actors Guild, I have to change my name. Not because it sounds ethnic, but because it sounds so perfectly generic that someone else in the union is already using it. While I'm at it, I change it completely, first name, last name, even the initial in the middle. I erase my identity and pull a new one from thin air. For months after, I keep forgetting who I am.

I begin to sleep with men who tell me I remind them of someone, their daughter or their old girlfriend or someone they can't quite place. In actuality, they've seen me on television, selling credit cards and peanut butter and cough syrup. If not a star, I do well enough to incur envy. My agent returns my calls. I make money. I spend it. I spend some more. When I've had a stressful day, I leaf through mailorder catalogues. It soothes me, the glossy photos of chinos and anoraks and polos, the people wearing them who look vaguely like me, maybe a little happier. I call a 1-800 number and order sweaters, in celery, in cactus, in dusk. I meet someone and we drink blue margaritas.

Given all this, this surfeit of normalcy, how to explain the eight months when I cannot get out of bed? How to explain the inarticulate terrors of morning, the black slumps round about four? I cannot trust my own judgment on such matters, so I follow the masses wending their way into therapy.

The first session, she asks about my family. She invites them into the room, and they come piling in. They take up every chair and nudge me over on the couch. We're all uncomfortable, but we make an effort. When asked to confront our inner workings, we try. We tell what may be the truth, what we think she'd like to hear, and we wonder if we are boring her. She believes us to be hedging, resisting the awful secret truths of her calling. We fumble to oblige her, we search for something that sounds original and genuine, we weep in frustration.

At last, through the graces of a new movement, we are given the words to express our emptiness. We are the soul-murdered children of blank-aholics. We love too much. We have past lives more colorful than this one. We are each of us creative. We are each of us unique. We decide to become Native American. We remember a Sioux ancestor back there somewhere. We buy bundles of sage and turquoise-studded bracelets. We dance with wolves. We feel our shape shift, our history elide. We're back in the saddle again.

ANOTHER LITTLE PIECE

It was silly to feel what she was feeling, Elaine told herself. She was forty-nine, too old to be an orphan.

Elaine had just spent another afternoon and evening at her mother's. After four weekends of sorting and packing, they had worked their way down to the basement, the midden where for several decades the family had carted and dumped all artifacts no longer used but of some dubious value. Her mother was paring down; she had sold the house and bought a condo in Durham.

"What about these?" Elaine asked, holding up a pair of cow salt-and-pepper shakers she remembered from her childhood.

Her mother gave them hardly a glance. "Goodwill."

"How about this?" Wrapped in yellowed tissue was a ceramic crèche that had appeared on the front hall table every December for decades.

"Goodwill."

And so on and so on, through boxes of old vacation slides and photo albums, a croquet set, canning jars, souvenir ashtrays and spoon rests, a rock tumbler for polishing agates, high school yearbooks, the linen christening gown she and her brothers had been baptized in, the old brown sleeping bags with deer and ducks on the flannel lining.

And then her father's metal tackle box. Elaine found it in the growing sprawl of To Go items. Each tray was neatly labeled in her father's hand and filled with flies and hooks and flashers, spools of thread and bits of line.

"You're not really thinking of throwing this away?" Elaine urged.

"I can't imagine what I'm going to do with fishing tackle. Somebody else might as well get some good out of it."

"It's not as though you're going into the Witness Protection Program, Mom," Elaine snapped. "You don't have to leave it all behind."

"I'm trying to do you a favor, missy. When I die, you won't have to feel guilty about throwing things away. I only wish my own mother had done this. Do you know I found boxes and boxes of used lightbulbs in the attic? All the filaments burned out. She hadn't thrown out a lightbulb in twenty years."

"There's a difference."

"It's all just stuff," her mother pronounced, and that was that.

So Elaine ended up feeling guilty about the boxes of rescued history she carried to her car at the end of the day. It was mostly sentimental junk; still, her mother's breezy disregard prickled her nerves. She had spent the day trying to be an adult and failing, and now she was tired and grimy. A quick stop at the store, then she was going to go home, make herself a grilled cheese sandwich, take a shower, and go to bed.

And that was when she saw her ex. At that moment, Neil was sailing his cart through the brightly lit produce section, checking a list against the rows of polished and misted fruit, squinting in concentration, his tongue thrust into his cheek. Typically, he was oblivious to everything except the task in front of him. He threw a dozen oranges into a bag and then strode to a pyramid of corn, where he began ripping back husks and tossing the imperfect ears aside.

She noticed others watching him, too. He was still handsome, but not movie-star handsome. In photographs, he might easily be overlooked. But people gravitated to Neil. His confidence was magnetic. He was a pied piper, at the forefront of countless fads that had washed across Eastlake over the years. She had seen it happen again and again. Neil had been the first person in their neighborhood to take up cross training and the first one to throw it over for free weights. Later there was Rollerblading and touring the wine countries by bicycle.

When they were young, Elaine had been afraid he would die of a heart attack before he was thirty and leave her widowed with two small children. She had never known anyone with so much energy. He might get called in on an emergency in the middle of the night, and still see two dozen patients the next day. Then he'd come home, take the edge off with a five-mile run before dinner, and *she* was the one who was exhausted, having spent the day following a toddler around the house. In his wake, she always felt tired and inferior. Eventually, she had drifted to the rear of the conga line and been replaced by a younger, sturdier model who needed less sleep.

Already, there was a knot forming around the bin of corn.

She didn't feel up to talking to him tonight, so she decided to skip the tomatoes she had come in for and headed toward the frozen desserts aisle instead.

In the first months after the divorce, she had avoided their old restaurants, the drugstore, the dry cleaner, anywhere they might cross paths. She avoided the neighborhood where he'd built a new house, and kept a sharp eye peeled for his BMW and the little red Miata his girlfriend, Nicole, drove. Even so, they lived in a small community and she bumped into him now and again. A year later, she had more or less grown used to it, although she was surprised she hadn't seen his car in the supermarket parking lot.

They were out of Chunky Monkey. She was reaching into the smoking interior of the ice cream case when she heard her name at her back. Neil was behind her, his cart filled to the brim. He looked pleased to see her, although she could tell from the way he furtively appraised the carton of Chocolate Mint in her hand that he was making an effort not to lecture her on fats. He made a generous living replacing arteries.

"What do you know? I never would have picked you out as a night shopper." His smile was broad and innocent.

"How are you, Neil?"

"I'm fine," he said, as always, but there was an unfamiliar hesitancy in his voice. She ignored it. She had her own problems. Besides, she probably already knew his. Their children kept her abreast. Nicole had skipped town back in March and, according to the credit card statements that still came to Neil's house, had returned to California.

"Have you tried this?" he asked. He had moved to the far side of the aisle where the fresh yogurt machine stood. He was filling a Styrofoam tub from the nozzle marked Raspberry Swirl. "This is my favorite flavor. And you don't even have to feel guilty."

"I like my guilty pleasures."

He smiled, good-natured but puzzled. "You don't know what you're missing. I eat this every night. Here, taste." He squirted a little onto a plastic spoon.

"No, thanks."

"C'mon, just a taste." He held out the spoon as though he were trying to tempt a fussy infant.

"I don't like yogurt." Her voice was sharp, and a shopper glanced in their direction.

He blinked, startled. She watched a tide of hurt surprise ripple across his face. And then it was gone.

"Okay." He shrugged and tossed the spoon into a trash receptacle. "But I'm telling you, this stuff is really good." He smiled, forgiving her, then snapped a lid on his container of yogurt and tossed it onto the heap of bagged fruit and vegetables in his cart.

She hadn't seen Neil's car in the supermarket lot because it wasn't there. When she came through the sliding doors with her bag of toilet paper, milk, bread, and tomatoes (she had relented, after all, relinquishing the ice cream), Neil was pacing across the lot, talking into his cell phone. He waved and Elaine tossed him a wave back, but then he began loping toward her.

"Elaine, my car's gone."

"Gone?"

Eventually it came out that he had left the doors unlocked and the keys in the ignition, but as he explained to the policeman when he arrived, he parked the car right at the front door and he was inside for only ten minutes, fifteen at the outside. The officer was courteous, taking down the license and make of the car.

"You can come in tomorrow and file a report. Do you have a way to get home?"

"I've got a load of groceries." Neil gestured to a cart stuffed with bags and abandoned in the dark asphalt sea. "Elaine?"

She nodded.

"My wife'll give me a lift."

Neil wasn't upset about the car so much as bemused. "It's not like this is a bad neighborhood." He was waiting for her to agree.

"I never could understand why you took chances like that," she said. "You act like the universe will suspend the rules for you."

"Five minutes. That's just plain dumb to steal a car parked right in front of the door."

They drove in silence for a few blocks, just the radio buzzing some tune too low to register, the hum of the car's engine. She searched for some neutral conversational topic— the threatened nurses' strike, the new stadium that was going up—but every subject she tested in her mind sounded false against the quiet. Neil, on the other hand, seemed comfortable. The intimacy of that annoyed her unreasonably.

"I'm not your wife anymore, you know."

He looked at her blankly.

"You told the policeman I was your wife."

"Did I?" He grinned. "Do you want to go back and set him straight?"

They stopped at a traffic signal and waited for a ridiculously long time, the only car at the intersection, while the ghosts of daytime traffic were ushered through.

"Maybe it'll turn up," she said.

"Yeah, I suppose so."

She sensed his attention had shifted. His mind was onto something else and he was waiting for her to redirect the conversation, to pry loose his thoughts with a series of deft questions. This had been their pattern. Elaine resisted.

The light changed, and they drove through downtown. At night, it looked like a scene from a science fiction movie, silent and swept clean of humanity. The wide streets were deserted, traffic signals washing the empty pavement green, then yellow, then red. Warning lights winked from the tops of dark office towers, all jutting mirrored surfaces. A few squat buildings remained from the days when this was still a bedroom community. The old 76 filling station on the northeast corner was a video store now, its fluorescent interior spilling white light onto a row of empty parking spaces. Kitty-corner from the filling station was the Eastlake Savings and Loan where they'd taken out the loan for the second house; it was now a branch of one of the big interstates, but it looked more or less the same, smaller against the backdrop of high-rises.

Elaine finally relented. "The kids told me about Nicole. I'm sorry." The funny thing was, she truly was sorry. She could remember predicting bitterly that he would someday realize what a flimsy piece of packaging he'd traded her in for, all spandex and peroxide, but now that she'd been proven right, it gave her no pleasure.

"Did they tell you she's suing me for support?"

"Can she do that?"

"Nothing to stop her from trying, I guess." He shook his head, with a kind of rueful bewilderment. "No fool like an old fool, right?" He seemed to be actually asking her the question.

"Do you want me to contradict you?"

"Well, you could tell me I'm not so old." He smiled wooingly.

In spite of herself, she smiled back. "Face facts, Neil. You're an old goat."

Somehow that satisfied him. He nodded, oddly pleased.

"Do you remember what we paid for the house on Phinney?" he asked.

"Thirty-seven thousand."

"I drove by there last month. It's on the market. Just out of curiosity, I called up the realtor. They were asking three twenty for it."

"You're joking." She was continually shocked by how fast things changed.

"That was a cute little house."

It had been the first of three houses, just four doll-sized rooms but with a wide covered porch and an old maple that shaded their bedroom with dancing green light. Darcy had been conceived in that room, and then slept in the bottom drawer of the dresser because there was no space for a crib. They would throw impromptu parties, half a dozen interns and their wives or girlfriends drinking sangria and dancing in the yard. Elaine felt a dull pang in her chest, something like grief for her child-husband and her younger self, the two of them bumbling and careless and, for a long while, lucky.

She passed the high school and the park and the Methodist church and then turned right into the neighborhood where Neil lived now. She found his driveway and left the engine running.

"Have you had dinner?" he asked.

"It's after eleven," she said, as if this were an answer. In truth, she rarely sat down to a meal, just threw one of those little frozen pizzas in the microwave or nibbled at whatever was handy. It was a holdover from being married to a doctor. When the kids were little, she had fought to keep their dinnertimes regular, but it often meant she had cooked dinner in two shifts and picked in between.

"Well, how about a glass of wine or something?"

"I've got to get home and get this stuff in the fridge."

"You can put it in mine. I hate eating alone," he added.

She was curious.

The extra house key was hidden under a pot next to the back door, exactly where anyone would look first. They entered the kitchen through the back door, and when Neil flipped on the lights, Elaine blinked in the sudden glare.

Every surface gleamed antiseptically under bright fixtures: an enormous stainless-steel gas range, a matching Sub-Zero refrigerator, double steel sinks deep enough to bathe a large dog in, frosted glass cabinets with metal pulls. What had surely been touted as modern and functional instead screamed "operating arena." Elaine could almost picture patients being prepped on the granite slab countertop of the island. He could bring his work home.

"Wow," she said stupidly.

"Do you like it?" he asked, and she was surprised to see that he wanted her approval.

"It's pretty impressive," she nodded.

"I've gotten into cooking," he said. "Mostly stir-fry and grilling, but I make my own marinades." He had the doors of the behemoth Sub-Zero opened wide and was unloading his groceries.

"Better get that ice cream in the freezer," he said, taking her grocery bag.

"I changed my mind on the ice cream. Just milk." He looked pleased.

"So, what do you say to some sautéed chicken breast, maybe a little pasta?"

"Really, just a glass of wine is fine. I can't stay long. I spent the day helping my mom pack up her house and I need a shower. I'm pretty filthy."

"I wasn't going to say anything." He grinned, but then quickly added, "You look great, Elaine. Really." He smiled.

This was new, a carefulness with her feelings that she wouldn't have credited him with.

"Here, sit." He gestured to a bar stool on the far side of the island. "Pinot grigio okay? I'll make a little extra chicken. Once you smell the garlic, you'll change your mind. So Polly's moving?"

She sat back with her glass of wine and watched as he piled ingredients onto the countertop, pulled down a sauté pan and pasta pot from the overhead rack, and set the water on to boil. A few sips of wine and the tightness she'd been feeling all day began to unravel.

"She's on a tear. You remember her china? Blue rims with little birds and berries?" But no, of course he wouldn't. "Sixteen place settings of Haviland and she was ready to haul it off to Goodwill."

Neil selected a chef's knife from a butcher block and began expertly mincing garlic. "Did you take it off her hands?"

"I'm putting it in storage. Darcy may want it when she gets settled."

He smiled good-naturedly. "Don't hold your breath, Elaine." Their daughter was living with a bunch of people in a farmhouse outside of Eugene, Oregon. She had spent the previous year living in trees for their own protection. It was their daughter's form of rebellion to actually live out the ideals of the sixties, in contrast to her parents who had merely smoked a little pot and feigned the styles.

"Well, tomorrow's the last day, then we're done. Except for the sideboard. I have to find some movers to take it to my house." She felt self-conscious when she referred to the house as hers. "You can't believe the estimates I've been getting just to haul one sideboard and a couple of chairs across town."

"Do you need a hand?" he asked. "Michael and I could rent a truck."

She answered reflexively. "Oh, no, I'll figure something out."

"I have to rent something to drive anyway. Might as well be a truck. I could pick it up in the morning, swing by Polly's after I stop at the police station." Neil was reaching for the phone, pressing a number on the speed dial. "I'll give Michael a call, see if he's free."

"It's almost midnight. Really, this isn't . . ."

"It's Saturday night. What do you think, I'm going to wake him up?" He wedged the phone between his shoulder and ear, and sliced the chicken breast into strips as he talked. "Hey. It's your old man." He was talking to Michael's voice mail. "If you're not doing anything in the morning, I could use your help. Someone made off with my car, and I promised your mother we'd help her move some furniture from Polly's. Shouldn't take more than an hour or so. I'll be up for a while. Give me a call."

It was Neil's habit to lowball the time involved in doing anything. He never allowed for traffic or missed turns, for checkout lines or the myriad of obstacles that could spring up. He saw only the unimpeded flow of his will. She, in turn, had always overcompensated by anticipating every roadblock. Right now, for instance, she could imagine with perfect clarity the phone call she'd get tomorrow: Neil explaining that he'd been held up by mysterious forces, the rental car agency that had rented every truck off the lot before his arrival, the desk sergeant who needed more paperwork filled out. Of course, it would only be a few more minutes and then he'd be on his way. Fifteen minutes, tops.

She knew him better than he knew himself. She could predict what he would order off a menu. She knew his habits and secret vanities, the way he squinted when he looked in the mirror, the way he could disappear into a project and not hear what was around him, not the babies crying, or later, the boom boxes thumping in the upstairs bedrooms. She knew the kind of jokes that made him laugh, the strangled cry he made when he climaxed, how he was always a little sheepish afterward.

She let the last swallow of wine roll around in her mouth and slide warmly down her throat.

He was the same man, and yet he wasn't. The entire time they'd been married, he'd never made anything more complicated than a sandwich, and here he was, testing a strand of pasta from the pot, sifting chopped basil and pine nuts over the chicken. She wondered how else he had changed.

The food was good. She had another glass of wine, and she talked about her mother's defection to North Carolina, and he talked about a trip he'd recently taken to Phoenix for a convention that had been heavily attended only because it was February and Phoenix was warm in February. They exchanged opinions about Michael's new girlfriend and agreed that this one seemed good for him, not like the last one. And they reminisced, like old friends who haven't seen each other in years. He had forgotten, until she mentioned it, the three months his crazy aunt lived with them. Poor thing, she really was crazy, not just an expression. They shouldn't laugh, but did he remember how they found the coffee can half-full of pee under her bed? And Daisy, the pet goat. What had they been thinking? The constant bleating and the damn thing ate a thousand dollars' worth of landscaping before they'd found a home for it.

Was it Banff where they'd cooked up the idea of getting a little dairy goat? It was that old man, the caretaker, and his stories about the health benefits of goat's milk. He would come by the cabin on some pretext, always in the late afternoons, and hang around telling them yarns about cougars and grizzlies until Neil invited him to stay for dinner. What a character. The trip had ended badly, though. They had been there a little less than five days when Michael found a yellow jacket nest.

"You remember? He swelled up like one of those balloons in the Macy's parade." Neil shook his head in wonder.

One minute Michael had been screaming and the next he was turning blue. Elaine would never forget how calm

Neil had been when he told her to hold the boy still while he punctured his throat. He needs air, Neil had said. She had screamed at him, called him a bastard and who knows what else, all the while desperately trying to wrench her baby away from him.

"Man, you were a she-cat," Neil laughed.

Elaine smiled, but the memory filled her with shame. "I didn't trust you," she admitted.

He stopped and looked at her and took this in, his eyebrows lifting in surprise. "I would never have let anything happen to Michael."

She nodded. "I know. Nevertheless."

Every day of their marriage, patients had turned their lives over to Neil. He had split them open at the sternum, taken hold of their beating hearts, and they had adored him for it. She had envied them their faith, the look she had seen in their eyes when they introduced themselves later in a restaurant or a store. "Your husband is an amazing man," they'd say. "But I guess you know that."

Tears sprang up in her eyes and she pressed them back with her fingers, shaking her head at her foolishness.

"When we split up, I realized I'd been bracing for it for years," she said. "When Jody and Hal separated. And then Kris Little, the Dali guy that used to work at the gallery. He dragged himself around like a dog that's been hit and left in the road. And I was thinking, when the time comes . . . I don't know what I was thinking, not that it wouldn't happen to us but that I was going to manage it better." She closed her eyes and exhaled jaggedly. "I mean, I loved you, but I just held a little in reserve, you know?"

He reached over and tentatively rested a hand on her back. He stroked her hair, smoothed the back of her neck. "I loved you, too." His voice was soft and hoarse.

The moment was suddenly taut. His hand slowed, feathering across her skin, leaving trails of heat. Elaine felt herself suspended from a great height and she willed herself to fall.

And then they were kissing. Their mouths and their hands remembered. He squeezed her hand and pulled her to her feet. She followed him through a dark, high-ceilinged living room and up an open staircase with cable railings like a ship's, and she had the sensation of being at sea, the taste of salt, a swaying unsteadiness in the rolling dark.

A phone was ringing in the dark and then the voice of her husband was speaking to someone, something about a car. For a long, reeling moment, she panicked, seeing the crumpled bodies of her children smashed against a windshield. Neil's voice was measured, no hint of alarm.

"Is it the kids?" she breathed.

"What?" He had hung up the phone. "Oh, yeah, probably a bunch of kids out for a joyride." He switched on a reading lamp and swung out of bed. "They didn't get far. The cops found it in the high school parking lot. The front left fender is banged up pretty good."

His car. The world righted itself again, and she found herself in an unfamiliar bed. The sheets smelled of bleach. Neil was pulling on shorts and jeans and socks.

"I'm just going to walk over and get it," he said.

"Now?" It was late, still dark outside.

"I don't want it towed unless it's necessary, and I hate to leave it sitting there. Go back to sleep." He leaned over and brushed his lips across her eyelids and her mouth. She felt her nipples harden against the starchy sheets and wondered idly if she should be feeling something else. And then he was gone. She heard a door somewhere in the house bump shut.

It was quiet, just the electric hum of a suburban night, but she couldn't sleep. She saw that her clothes were strewn across the flat expanse of carpet in a trail leading to the bed. The bedroom had the same elegant blankness as a hotel suite, right down to the big television screen recessed into the far wall. Below and on either side of the TV, barely visible seams outlined what must be drawers and closet doors. She got out of bed, lurching just a little as she stood. She was pleasantly woozy with sleep or wine. There were no latches or door handles, so she began bumping the wall in different spots with the palm of her hand. She listened. Nothing. And again, nothing. It was like being a safe cracker—she could be in one of those sixties caper movies. She wasn't aware of looking for anything in particular. A cabinet door clicked open. Inside were shelves with stereo equipment, drawers of CDs and videotapes. In the dim light, she made out titles of exercise videos and several recent movies. She recognized Neil's hand in the selection of music, mostly CDs he had taken with him when he moved out. He had stopped paying attention to music after college, and so his tastes were frozen back in the Monterey and Motown period. When he'd hum tunes around the house or sing in the shower, it was always thirty-year-old songs and he'd make up his own words. She wondered if Nicole had even known he was changing the lyrics or if she thought there really were Dylan songs called "Mr. Tangerine Man" and "Knockers on Heaven's Door," if she thought the Beatles sang "When I'm Six-Foot-Four." She wondered if he'd put on Al Green when they made love.

Another click and a closet presented itself. She walked inside and found a light switch. The closet was organized into a neat geometry of hanging rods and shelves and drawers, like a Mondrian painting if the artist had worked in shirts and shoes instead of oils. She pulled out drawers containing balls of socks and stacks of T-shirts, familiar laundry interspersed with newer items she didn't recognize. She ran her hand down the row of suits, fingering the shoulders of the jackets.

At the end of the row, in the corner, she found women's clothing, what Nicole had left behind. A backless sundress. A pair of crushed velvet stretch pants. A silky short kimono, black with a purple bleach stain on the sleeve. A couple pairs of jeans, a striped boatneck sweater. A pink T-shirt that said BRAT in glitter across the front.

She stared at the clothing, breathed in the weight of its physical presence. Her mother was wrong about its being just stuff. Years from now, she thought, this is what will tell them how we lived.

She held up the T-shirt and then pulled it over her head, tugging the fabric down over her chest. She squeezed into the velvet stretch pants, wriggling them up over her hips. Then she pulled the kimono off its hanger and put it on. When she turned around and found the mirror on the back of the closet door, she stared for a long time at her image. The woman reflected back was bedraggled, her hair wild with tangles, mascara smeared under her keening eyes. But it was something about the ill-fitting clothes, the garish pink over her loose breasts and the long sweep of the kimono sleeve when she brushed the hair out of her eyes. They transformed her into someone else. Not Nicole. It took a moment before the name fell into place.

She looked like Janis Joplin, better than that, Janis if she'd fallen in love and gotten married and had children, if she'd survived long enough to know that nothing ended the way it does in songs. Come, go, a marriage didn't dissolve completely: they were still each other's history, as permanent as ink stains.

Elaine was singing, impersonating Joplin's guttural rasp. It was exhilarating to bring this howl up from her gut. She let her hair fall back into her face and wailed out lyrics she remembered from when she and Neil were young, when giving away your heart had seemed like a simple thing to do. She sang another line, then changed the words. Just bake it! Bake another little pizza, you tart, now, baby. Elaine took a sweeping bow. Thank you. Thank you.

ROMANCE MANUAL

After a blizzard in New Haven, three slushy weeks in Pittsburgh, and more of the same in Cleveland, the sudden flush of heat in Sarasota is unreal. So far as I can tell, though, this is the only draw here, the tropical sun. Other points of interest: Sarasota is the winter home of the Ringling Brothers Circus. Period. The streets are empty except for a few old folks riding golf carts and oversized tricycles. Pelicans waddle across the docks and flop into the cobalt water. Clown Paradise. Even the theater we're playing is painted a ridiculous purple.

I waste the afternoon alone by the motel pool, reading a romance novel. It's hard to believe someone actually gets paid to write this shit. I could do better. Take my own life for instance: make an adjustment here and there (edit out Pittsburgh, lose Akron) and presto, every hausfrau's fantasy.

(It was a glamorous theatrical tour. Each new city beck-oned with promises, whispered of romance, drew her name in its lights.)

I'm waiting for Pavel, taking a flier that he might show up for a swim, but the place feels abandoned, deservedly so. The bottom of the pool is mottled with dead leaves, and rick-ety aluminum chairs creak in the breeze. Another Holiday Inn hell, courtesy of the tour managers back in New York. But when I close my eyes, the heat on my skin feels the same as Tahiti, like Fiji or Bali or Bora-Bora.

(She was alone in an unspoiled paradise, the beach as fresh as white linen, not a footprint but hers in the sparkling sand.)

I haven't been to any of those places, but I expect they never live up to the fantasy. After my old college roommate caught her husband bonking one of his clients, they went on a second honeymoon to St. Bart's. A fresh start and all that. A postcard turned up in my mail showing an incredible beach fringed with palms trees and lapped by an improbably sapphire sea. On the back was a phony-looking postmark and my friend's cryptic comments on the rain. They were divorced four months later.

(She picked a conch shell off the beach and held it to her ear. She thought she heard low laughter, and when she looked up, she saw a handsome stranger.)

When I wake, my knees are shrimp-colored. Before I go to the theater I rub myself with ice cubes. By curtain call, my skin is aflame.

*   *   *

The others have scouted out a joint that serves cheap margaritas and plates of alligator fingers. Pavel will be there. I gingerly slip off my third-act costume; the brocade scratches like sandpaper. I peel away my eyelashes, smear off my face with cold cream, pull pins out of my hair. In the glare of the caged bulbs ringing the mirror, I look like Bozo's girlfriend: red and puffy, with clownish white triangles over my eyes, my crotch, and each tit. Never in my life have I managed a tan, only freckles and burns. I carefully reline my eyes and mouth and thank the gods that cocktail lounges are dark.

(His eyes searched the smoky café, looking for the mysterious redhead who had so captivated him that afternoon on the beach.)

When I packed my trunk in New York, the only heat was spitting out of a radiator, but even so, how much foresight would it have taken to tuck in something slinky and cool? I change into black leggings and a "Virginia Is For Lovers" T-shirt, and stand back from the mirror. The reflection is not what one would hope for—I look like a tourist signed up for the wrong package. I add a red chiffon scarf, knotting it around my hips to draw attention to one of my better features. Not subtle, but if you want to catch a fish, use the shiny lure.

(In the far corner he spotted her, as cool and alluring as a mirage.)

I am determined not to go to bed alone tonight. Not that finding someone to fuck is a challenge; on the road, it's much easier than getting room service or extra towels, but, when possible, I prefer the semblance of romance. Romance requires more patience, laying the groundwork. I've been working on this one for weeks, creating opportunities to be swept away. I can't speak for the reality, but I like the illusion of falling in love.

Romance is always a gamble and, frankly, the odds are against you. But if you gamble long enough, you develop certain strategies: bluffing, waiting out the bad deals, trusting your intuition when it comes, whatever you think will shorten those odds. I picked out Pavel back in Cleveland. His name gave him a decided advantage over the rest of the males in the company. Pavel Milov. It's a Czech name, docked of all the extra k's and z's when he became an actor, but still exotic, a quality I prize highly. Sounds like a freedom fighter or an expatriate poet. Scratch the surface and they're all the same, but you learn not to scratch.

As it happens, the surface of Pavel is gorgeous. Not tall, but very sculpted, with a languid smile and eyes the green of beach glass. Maybe gorgeous is too much; he is definitely short and his nose is a tad beakish. He is also married, but I can overlook that. In fact, sometimes that can work in your favor. If you lose, they go back to their wives and you can tell yourself truthfully it was no reflection on you.

*   *   *

(When she stepped through the stage door, the perfume of bougainvillea and saltwater drifted out of the lush dark. The surf was as quiet and rhythmic as breathing.)

The door behind me screeches and thuds shut. It's Pavel. I don't believe in luck; I believe that people get what they deserve. I say "pretty night" like an invitation, and smile. I'm not going anywhere, got no plans. I brush an imaginary hair away from my cheek. His eyes dart back and forth, then he grabs my elbow and yanks me down a step, out of the light.

(His handsome features betrayed no emotion, but something in his manner hinted at danger.)

He says, "Let's go for a walk." I'll admit this is easier than I'd expected.

We slip around the back side of the theater and walk past the loading dock, toward the sound of the ocean. At the far corner of the building, he slows his pace and then stops.

"Come here," he says. He pulls me through a thicket of bushes and presses my back against the concrete wall. I feel his hands push up under my T-shirt and knead my sunburned flesh. I whimper, but it sounds convincingly like passion.

(When they kissed, her blood rose like warm water over her head.)

I'm not about to get laid in the bushes, so I loosen his grip on my tits and pull away ever so slightly, catching my breath. "I like the way you walk."

"Okay, we'll walk. It's a good mile back to the motel. I've got a pint of scotch in my room."

"Don't you think they'll miss us?" Like I care.

"I told them I had to get back and call home."

The dead palm fronds that litter the sidewalk rustle like paper in the warm breeze. Between blinding sweeps of head-lights, the sky is black overhead and dusty with stars. I'm feeling helium-light, my feet almost skipping. I kick at an empty beer can, sending it clattering on ahead. I want to throw out my arms and twirl, to make the stars spin.

(He swept her up in his strong arms. They whirled across the dance floor, and out onto the starlit balcony.)

You have to squint hard to endow the Sand Drift Motel with charm. It is a sagging pink stucco, parked on the main drag to pick off weary motorists. From a distance it looks vaguely festive, but up close the neon vacancy sign lurches drunkenly and the orange-lit plaster fountain is dry and caked with al-gae. When Pavel unlocks his door and snaps on the overhead light, any last fragments of illusion shrivel.

He quickly pulls shut the flimsy curtains. I make a bee-line for the ceramic lamp and then turn off the switch at the door. He is moving toward me, already fiddling with a but-ton on his shirt. So I say, "How about that drink you prom-ised me?" I don't like to be rushed.

I fetch two water glasses from the top of the toilet tank and unwrap them while he rummages through the suitcase spread open on one of the beds. I sit on the edge of the un-made bed and feign interest in a tourist guide put out by the local Chamber of Commerce. He fills my glass, stretches out next to me and we drink.

"Say something to me in Czech."

He laughs. "Oh God, you're kidding. I don't speak a word. I mean, a phrase or two, but nothing . . ."

"Whatever."

"Whatever. Okay. *'Jdi do prdele.'*"

"That's beautiful. What does it mean?"

"'Fuck off.' All I can remember are the obscenities. The others are worse; my grandfather was a randy guy."

Pavel is off on some story his grandfather told him about a prostitute. I settle back against the headboard and drink steadily until my body feels boneless and airy. Through the open window, there is splashing in the pool. The curtains billow slightly, ballooning the faded cotton orchids and making the hula girls sway. I swallow another mouthful of the scotch and follow its heat threading down my middle, out my limbs.

My voice sounds far away. "Do you do this all the time?"

"He says this to a nine-year-old kid." Pavel is still rattling on about grandpa. "What's that?"

"Do you do this all the time? Seduce women up to your room."

"Oh." He smiles. "Only the beautiful ones."

"And have there been a lot of beautiful women?"

"Not like you."

I'm not beautiful, but it doesn't matter. We will pretend that I am. One arm slides around me and the other clicks off the lamp on the nightstand. Blue light from the pool ripples across the walls.

At first I watch myself from a distance, guiding my hands, tilting my throat back, scoring like music the gasps and the moans. But gradually I fall under the spell of my own acting or the rhythm of the act, it doesn't matter which. I have forgotten myself for a while.

(The passion they had hidden exploded like a volcano and swept them along in its current. She had never imagined it could feel like this.)

We lie in the blue shadows, stretched out across the rubble of chlorine-smelling sheets and gritty bits of sand. Pavel gets up and goes into the bathroom, and I can hear him taking a leak. When he comes back to the bed, he passes me his water glass with its half-inch of warm scotch and I drain it. I run my fingers across the mat of damp curls on his chest.

I turn my face away from his and let my eyes fill with water. I have landed more than one part because I can produce real tears on cue. If the scene is well written, it happens on its own, like stepping out of my life and becoming the vision. If not, I think of my mother backing the station wagon over our cat, Buster, when I was nine. Tonight I'm on a roll and the tears feel genuine.

I wait for Pavel to feel the silence in the room, and then I inhale jaggedly. He lifts my chin in his hand, turns my face toward his, and asks me what's the matter. Nothing, I tell him, but he persists. Finally I say, in a shattered whisper, that

I'm afraid I could get too attached to him. He is surprised, but I can tell he doesn't doubt for a minute that this is possible. His drowsy eyes focus sharp, and tiny fissures crinkle across his brow.

It's risky to suggest consequences. They can panic, suddenly flash on the wife and kiddies back home and start backpedaling. On the other hand, feeling desired, even loved, is a powerful aphrodisiac. Who doesn't want that fantasy?

(He took her in his strong arms and whispered her name like a prayer. What they felt might be crazy, he said, but love was like that.)

"Well, I could get pretty attached to you, too. Especially if you keep doing that with your hand."

I'm drifting off when the phone rings, loud as an alarm. Pavel stretches out lazily for the receiver and cradles it against his shoulder while he lights a cigarette.

"No, I just walked in the door a few minutes ago." He snaps on the lamp, and I curl away from the light.

"Oh, not bad tonight. We had a full house. Pretty lively old farts, too. Better than the stiffs in Cleveland."

I draw a damp tangle of sheet up over my naked back and lie perfectly still. I'm listening for a nervous tremor or a false note in his voice, but it isn't there.

(He hated all this, the lies and deceptions. It tore him up inside to see her unhappy. But it would be different soon.)

"Well, maybe we should get somebody else to do it and deduct it from the rent. They've been dinking around . . ."

I lie there like a lump for a while, and then I go into the bathroom and sit. The john faces a mirror; in the fluorescent light my sunburn looks freshly slapped. My shoulders are starting to peel away in patches. I shift onto the tile floor. From this angle, the shower stall seems to tilt precariously over me. I count blooms of mildew up on the ceiling. The sickening light and the glare off the white tiles remind me of the places they put nutcases.

I tell myself that they're talking about plumbing, for God's sake, the kind of business you transact with a wife. This has nothing to do with me, with us. When he gets her off the phone, I'll suggest a dip in the pool.

(How could he forget that night in Sarasota when they swam naked and unashamed, watched only by the stars overhead?)

The door is ajar; through the slit I can make out his profile, the Roman nose, half a drowsy smile, the green eye gazing far away. He is still talking. "It was eighty-two today. . . . Just went to the beach for a while. Remember at Nag's Head, all the old guys lined up fishing blues off the pier? I think they come down here for the winter. . . . That was good, wasn't it?" A long pause. "Me too, babe. Good night."

The phone clicks into the receiver. I hear him yawn, and then he shuts off the lamp.

He's forgotten I'm here.

I wait a few moments, unsure of my next move, then decide that the best course of action is to act as though nothing has happened. I emerge from the bathroom, spraying an arc of light across the bed that catches Pavel like a deer in headlights. One hand sneaks over his flaccid genitals.

"Home?" I ask brightly.

He nods, blinking against the light.

"So, how about a swim?" I suggest.

"It's kind of late. Maybe tomorrow, huh?"

"Tomorrow we go to Tulsa."

"Yeah. Well . . ." His eyes shift away, to the door. "It's kind of late."

When I was eleven, my family went on vacation to Lincoln City on the Oregon coast. I met a boy, Jeff was his name, and we spent long days on the beach, daring each other into the chill green surf, feeling the pull of the undertow slide around our ankles as we raced back out. Lying side by side on beach towels, we would talk and pretend not to notice when the tips of our fingers brushed the other's skin. Our families teased us, said it was puppy love. On the morning my family was leaving, Jeff led me by the hand into a dune behind the motel parking lot, and he kissed me. We were as solemn as penitents taking communion. Then he said that he loved me and would not forget me, not ever. All the way back to Sacramento, I kept my face pressed to the car window, feeling the chrysalis of my heart crack open, a strange lush ache. I pretended it was carsickness, but my mother knew. There will be others, she told me.

Meanwhile, tomorrow we go to Tulsa. I pick up my T-shirt, puddled on the carpet, and pull it over my head. I drag on my pants, stuff my underwear in a pocket. My scarf is nowhere to be seen, but so what, I've lost things before. At the door, I turn and smile brightly at him.

"Sweet dreams, lover."

THE BEST MAN

Mike follows a trail of bright pink spots. They lead into the living room, across the carpet, and to the off-white couch he and Rachel bought before they became parents. There lies his son, sucking on his sippy cup, blissful as a junkie. Somehow, Noah has managed to spill juice out of the cup, something the manufacturer claims is impossible but which Noah accomplishes with astonishing regularity.

"Shit, Noah." Mike is yelling. "Is it too much to ask to leave us one fucking"—he corrects himself—"one frigging room?"

His son stares at him, stricken, his wide eyes already brimming with tears.

"Just give me that." Mike takes the plastic cup, and Noah lets out a wail.

"We've talked about this. No juice in the living room." He tries reasoning, but the boy is inconsolable, lost in his grief. "Okay, c'mon, we can finish it in the kitchen." Mike starts to pick up his son, but the pitch of the squall rises. Walk away, Mike tells himself. Just walk away. He goes into the kitchen and returns again with spot remover and a sponge. Mike tries to ignore his son's sobs as he scrubs at the carpet. It is unendurable.

"Hey, I've got an idea. Why don't you show me how your new fire truck works. What do you say?" Mike is almost pleading.

Noah stops howling and appraises Mike warily. The boy's cheeks are still slick with tears and snot, but the storm is already over. He trots toward his bedroom, and when Mike catches up, Noah is waiting to demonstrate how the ladder raises and lowers, how the red light flashes, how the truck can scale the bookcase and walls of his room. Just like that, another twenty minutes have passed.

Mike leaves his son herding plastic farm animals up the ladder of the toy fire truck, and checks again the slow progress of his wife's dressing. The babysitter is fifteen minutes late and Rachel is still half-dressed, sifting through a heap of panty hose on the bed. She runs her hand through each leg and holds it up to the light, appraising the nylon with the concentration of a jeweler looking for flaws.

She is wearing a lace bra and matching panties, less familiar than the cotton underthings she usually wears. Her breasts and buttocks billow out of the skimpy lace, and Mike can almost feel in his fingertips the swells and hollows of her flesh. It feels like the itch of a missing limb. Now's a bad time for this train of thought, he tells himself. Now usually is. They had a hard time conceiving Noah, and the three years of calendars and thermometers and injections left the hardened imprint of obligation on their lovemaking. Even after the triumph of their son's birth, they approach each other measuredly.

Mike checks his watch: 2:35.

"Why don't you throw them out if they have runs in them?"

"Not runs, snags. If I threw out a pair of panty hose every time they had a snag, I'd wear them once."

"Then wear them once," he snaps. He snatches a pair off the bed and lobs them into the wastebasket.

"Mike, those are four-fifty a pair. What's with you today?"

I'm going crazy, he thinks. He's not, but he wants to. What he would give for one day, just one, when he could blow it through the roof, get drunk, sleep with a stranger, and not live with the consequences. One day, and then he'd come back. Happily. It's not that he doesn't love Rachel and Noah. He would crawl over glass for them. But just one day.

He can't tell Rachel all this, though: the price of being given a second chance is that for the rest of his life he will weigh his words and be careful not to do anything irrevocable.

He retrieves the stockings, but she's already found a pair to her liking and is stretching the filmy material up the length of each calf.

"I'm sorry. I'm feeling squirrelly today."

Rachel bounces on her toes, tugging the waistband up over her buttocks. "You're nervous about seeing your old girlfriend." She says this as calmly as stating the time of day. Even as he is denying it, Mike realizes that his mind is as familiar to Rachel as her body is to him.

The babysitter finally shows. Mike watches his son gallop down the hall and thrust the toy fire truck into the girl's hands. The boy's eyes are round and hopeful, like an eager suitor's. He tugs at her knee, trying to scale the leg of her jeans, until she absently scoops him up. Mike tries to imagine what is different about her from a string of rejected sitters, but there is nothing he can see that might account for his son's violent adoration. That's the way of it, he thinks. It's just there, inexplicable as electricity. He wonders again how it will be to see Caitlin.

While Rachel gives the sitter a few last-minute instructions about naps and fruit and phone numbers, Noah croons the girl's name and tries to seduce her away with Curious George videos. Mike wants to kiss his son good-bye, but he is clearly a fifth wheel. He remembers the tearful scenes that used to precede every exit. He's surprised to find he misses them.

"We'll bring you back a piece of cake," he offers.

"Don't push your luck," his wife whispers, and they slip out the door.

*   *   *

The Sunday afternoon traffic is stop-and-go. Mike pulls out around some moron trying to make a left turn on Flat-bush and has to lie on the horn and gun the sluggish engine just to get back into the left lane before he gets nailed. For all that, they get stuck at the light. He still misses his old Fiat, a spry little gem sacrificed on the altar of adulthood. Rachel hated it, insisted it made him drive like a maniac, but you have to drive aggressively in this city or you get crushed. Still, there was no arguing with the fact that a Fiat has no place for a car seat. He couldn't bring himself to trade it in, so for months after they bought the sedan with the four-wheel drive and the good safety rating, he continued to rise at dawn every other day and move his old love to the alternate side of the street. It came down to the fact that at sixteen he had thought a sports car would complete his life, and twenty-plus years later it was hard to let go of the idea.

They inch up the ramp onto the bridge. Sunlight flashes through the cable webbing of the spans, and Mike admires a ketch on the bay below. The sails arch taut, the boat heeled flat against the glittering water. He watches the boat skid to-ward the Verrazano Bridge, out to sea, and imagines the feel of lines pulling through his palms.

Mike double-parks in front of the restaurant, and Rachel comes around and burrows into the driver's seat, readjusting the mirrors.

"You sure you don't want to come in and watch the rehearsal?" he asks.

"No, Macy's is having a sale on OshKosh. Noah's outgrowing his old ones. I'll be back before six."

When Rachel pulls out into traffic, he turns and checks his reflection in the plateglass window. His face is still ruddy, a little tan left over from a weekend spent out at Montauk. Behind his glasses, pale lines splinter out from the edges of his eyes, like cracked glaze on pottery. There's also a little silvering at the temples that wasn't there when Caitlin last saw him. You could make a case that the gray hairs go with the suit and the tan. Makes him look successful, he decides. All in all, looking pretty good at thirty-eight, one of the last of his crowd who hasn't gotten thin on top or thick in the middle. The thought that Caitlin must also have changed snags at the edge of his mind, but he brushes it away, tucks his glasses into his breast pocket, and strides through the front door.

The restaurant is cavernous and cool, a former USO hall refurbished with yellow walls and large unframed canvases. Mike steps quickly through the bar and up into the main room. The tables have been cleared away and replaced with rows of chairs leading to a low platform swagged with ribbon and greens. A ponytailed man in leather jeans is standing on the platform, squinting up into the balcony over Mike's head. Suddenly music crashes through the room, a screeching burst of violins and then silence.

"Okay, okay, back it up and lower the volume a tad, hmm?" The man sees Mike and hops off the platform.

"I hope you're Michael. Oh, good, we're just about ready to do a quick run-through. We'll get this out of the way and let Andrea get dolled up. Phillip"—he serenades the balcony again—"the best man is here. Are you girls ready to go?"

Phil bounds down the metal stairs and lopes toward Mike. He looks different today. Mike can't place why, and then he realizes it's the suit. Phil's a musician who does carpentry on the side; his idea of dressing up has always been an old corduroy blazer on top of the jeans and cowboy boots. Today he is wearing a charcoal gray suit with an expensive Italian drape, a yellow silk tie, the whole nine yards. From the neck down, Phil is transformed, but the face is still too rugged for the costume. Mike is reminded of those photo booths at carnivals, the painted plywood scenes that you stuck your head into, your head on top of the body of a Victorian bathing beauty or an Old West cowboy.

Phil claps Mike on the back and then grins self-consciously, flinging his palms out and stepping back so Mike can take in the full effect.

"What d'ya think, man? I figured I'd dude up a little for the folks."

The man in the leather jeans is waving at them. "All right, front and center, boys. Is the music keyed up? Andrea, Caitlin, don't forget to pause on the bottom step for your photo op."

Handel's *Water Music* fills the empty restaurant. Mike stands next to Phil and peers up into the balcony, but he can't see Caitlin. He whispers a quick, "How ya doin'?"

"I feel like I walked into rehearsals for *A Chorus Line*."

"You got opening-night jitters?"

"Nah, I'm fine, really man. The way I see it, I married Andy six years ago. I just wanted to see what she looks like in a dress." Phil falters and tears blink in his eyes. He grins loopily. "I'm a happy guy, Mikey. What can I say?" Mike throws an arm around his shoulder and they clench each other, as awkward and passionate as teenagers.

Phil has always been a relatively happy guy. Mike envies him his easy luck. Phil never crossed over that invisible line. He's never had more than a bad hangover, never made mistakes he couldn't live with, never threw away something good when he had it.

The music cascades and the ponytailed man sings, "Okay, Caitlin, that's your cue." Without his glasses, Mike sees only a thin blurry figure wavering slowly down the stairs. Ten years blink away, and he recalls a riveting woman with Black Irish eyes and a mouth like a longshoreman's, and she is going to spend the night with him and then her life with him and then she decides better of it. "In case you haven't noticed, the fucking party's over," the mirage tells him. "It stopped being fun for everyone else a long time ago." And then she is gone.

The person coming down the stairs sharpens into focus like an ink drawing, something Japanese, a crane. The weightless line of her body, long fingers clasping an imaginary bouquet at her waist, the dark hair scissored short now. Her eyes are older, and the years have altered her in some other way that Mike can't pinpoint, but she is still fiercely attractive. Mike feels a stab of regret, sharper than it was when she left him.

He doesn't even remember her going. By that time, he was so obsessed with drinking himself to death, a man dredging frantically for the bottom, that he'd felt her absence only as the removal of some obstacle. Suddenly everything solid had dissolved underneath him and he'd felt the bleary rush of getting closer to death. One dizzy exhalation. When he hit bottom, in a lozenge-pink room at Smithers, he'd been surprised to hear she'd left town months ago, gone to Texas.

Caitlin glances up at him, or at him and Phil, he can't tell, but he pulls the corners of his mouth into a smile. He wishes only to float above this moment and see the pattern, see where he might have ended up if he'd made different choices. He hears trumpets and kettledrums.

"And now the bride. You look radiant, darling. That's right, now pause on the stair, let everyone admire you."

Mike's job, so far as he can remember, is to keep the groom from losing his nerve for another hour and a half. But Phil looks fine, loose-limbed and joking, trading Bloody Mary recipes with the bartender. Mike slips out of the conversation and goes looking for Caitlin. He knocks on a door next to the kitchen.

"Andrea? It's Mike. Can I steal a couple of aspirin?"

The door cracks open, and Caitlin peeks through. "She doesn't want anyone to see her before the ceremony. Bad luck. I told her that was just the groom, but . . ." She shrugs. "You still smoke? I'll trade you for a cigarette." She holds out two tabs of aspirin, and he shakes a cigarette out of his pack. He is fumbling with his lighter, but she takes it.

"Not in here."

And she is leading him through the kitchen, past cooks and waiters arranging shrimp and cheese and grapes on platters. His heart is pumping, and he grabs her hand, his own palm so sweaty that his grasp slips. He remembers the first night, leaving a party half in the bag, following her ass out to the elevator. He was like a trained seal, its nose swaying to the rhythm of a herring. God, but she had rhythm, swaying, flailing in the boozy dark. Caitlin opens a metal door and steps outside. What did he say that night? "I want to make you happy." What a joke. He thinks to himself that he needs a drink. He pauses and glances back at a waiter, tastes the bite of gin in his throat.

. . . accept the things I cannot change.

The words click on like a tape in his head, there unwilled. And pictures: Caitlin rigidly staring out a black window while a beady-eyed drunk, his evil twin, shrieks and rants behind her. Caitlin and the drunk being thrown out of a cab. The drunk coming out of a blackout with his penis wilted inside her.

He changes his mind on the gin and tonic and follows her through the door. They are standing a few feet in from the street, facing the back side of an office building that shares the alley. He scans the length of the alley, open to the next block on the far end. The wedding guests will be passing by soon. He and Caitlin might be spotted here. He tells himself he won't let anything happen, but he also hopes he's wrong. Already, long shadows are stretching in shafts across the street. The top several rows of office windows catch the last of the sunset like square embers. Caitlin lights the cigarette, another orange glow.

"How long you in town for?" His question hangs uncertainly in the air.

Caitlin hands the lighter to him. "I'm leaving in the morning."

"That's too bad."

Caitlin nods without conviction. "It's good seeing everybody, Andrea and Phil. And you. I'm glad you're doing so well, Michael. Andrea keeps me up on everybody."

"You should stay a few days and . . ." He can't finish the sentence. And what? Let me make you happy?

"I've got a meeting on Monday," she says.

"Hell, I've got meetings all week. You cancel them, reschedule. You should stick around. There's a new restaurant in Soho I've been meaning to try."

"I don't like it here anymore, Michael."

"What, you prefer Texas?" He says this jokingly, but honestly the idea seems incredible.

Caitlin laughs. He casually hoists an arm around her thin shoulder.

"Tell me about the life of a Texan beauty."

"It's not exciting, but I like it. I have a house with a yard and a vegetable garden. I have a golden retriever. Dagwood. We go for walks down to this bridge every evening. You should see it, Michael. At sunset, bats, hundreds of them, swoop out from under the bridge and funnel up into the sky. They look like a twister."

"I don't know, Cate, sounds pretty lonely to me." He feels the warmth of her skin under his fingertips. She seems to be missing his cues, the heat that Mike feels rolling off him in waves. Instead, she continues to talk about the bats, a subject immune to subtle redirection.

"No really, it's beautiful. They do this thing, like sonar. They fly inches apart, wing to wing, bouncing signals off each other. They can't see a thing, but it doesn't matter because they can feel the shape of everything."

"My son dressed as a bat last Halloween," he tells her. "He insisted on being a green bat, go figure. Rachel bought some green tights and sewed him green felt wings. We had to stand behind him at every neighbor's door and mouth 'bat' so they'd know."

Mike can recall every detail of that night: Rachel kneeling behind their son and safety-pinning the wings in place,

Noah's round little belly protruding between his tights and a remarkably tiny sweatshirt. Everything still so small. Noah had refused to change out of his costume after they got home, and had fallen asleep with the felt wings wrapped around him like a blanket. Mike and Rachel stood over him, watching his little chest rise and fall, his face smeared with chocolate and flushed pink with sleep.

Caitlin steps out of his clasp, drops her cigarette on the pavement and grinds it out with the toe of her shoe.

"He sounds like a sweet kid, Michael."

Her voice wrenches him back, and he is momentarily disoriented. Despite the mugginess of this evening, he feels chilled, as though a fever were breaking. And then the afternoon slowly comes into focus, each moment leading up to this one, frozen like tracks behind him. This is one of the rewards of sobriety, an uncomfortable clarity.

"Yeah, Noah is amazing. The whole thing, having a kid, I can't explain it." Mike has to struggle to remain in the moment. "I'm luckier than I deserve to be, Cate."

Caitlin grins and half turns toward the door. "You always were, you son of a bitch."

"I'm sorry." He wants to say something else, but he doesn't know what.

"I know, Michael. Get over it."

All of their friends are there. Mike stands next to Phil and looks out over all the faces he knows. He finds Rachel sitting over to the left, studying the program in her hand as though there might be a quiz later. He can tell by her carefully erect posture that she is being brave. A wrenching tenderness grips his throat, unexpected, half-forgotten. When he finally catches her eye, she smiles brightly. He tries to return her smile in such a way that she will read what he's thinking. You, he thinks. I swear it's you.

Caitlin sails forward up the aisle. Then Andrea. The judge says some words. In the presence of this loving community. This is an affirmation of life. What we do matters. Then there are the promises, in good fortune or in adversity, to seek with her a life . . . Mike doesn't remember saying those words himself, though he knows he did. But he does remember hearing Rachel say them and seeing in her eyes absolute surety and calm, a faith in him that bound him to her irrevocably.

He watches Phil and Andrea embrace, the moment stretching imperceptibly until it snaps back into real time. The room bursts into applause and laughter. He can see only dimly: flickering candles, the fluttering outlines of bodies rising. There is music again, plunging forward, triumphant, and then the bride and groom are swept into the crowd and everyone is swirling up the stairs. Mike steps into the vortex, searching blindly for his wife. She is there somewhere—he can feel her.

THE BODHISATTVA

You'll never guess who I bumped into yesterday. Your predecessor, Dr. Fletcher. I was walking Porkchop in the park. No makeup, my baggy sweats. The split second I recognized him coming down the path, my first instinct was to climb a tree and hide. I probably should have, but there's the problem of hoisting up a fat Pekingese. And it would be so typical for him to spot me up there, crouching on a limb like the Cheshire cat. Can't you see it? "Abby, what a surprise." I've humiliated myself enough with him, thank you very much.

I just told you how I felt, didn't I? I felt like climbing a tree. That seems pretty straightforward.

I'm sorry, I guess I'm feeling a little defensive today.

Get this, he's bought a place over near Flatbush Avenue. Small world and all that. I actually said that when we saw each other. I mean there're over two million people in the borough, why shouldn't he be one of them? But I was so flustered. You'd think, after all this time.

He sees me, he says, "Would you believe I was just thinking about you? How are you?" Which, coming from a shrink, is always a loaded question. No offense. And he squeezes my shoulder. Next thing I know I'm walking arm in arm with this man I haven't seen in two years. Three, come July twenty-third.

What do you mean, what did I do? I didn't do anything. What could I do? Scream for help? Help, this man was my shrink and now he wants me to talk to him? That's what you all get paid for, theoretically anyway. No, I just tried to act like an adult. I asked him about Bangkok. Turns out, there's not much call for shrinks there. The Thais don't talk about their feelings. Not out of a sense of decorum or rigidity, I gather, but they just don't see the point. Given my own experience, I can't help but admire the wisdom of that. And then the nail in the coffin for a psychotherapy practice, guilt is not a Buddhist concept. Karma takes care of that. He stayed a year and a half, counseling the American businessmen there, but it wasn't enough to make a go of it.

He said, "Everyone is happy there, so I had to come back to New York."

I was tempted to suggest that he has some kind of allergic reaction to happiness, but as I said, I was trying very hard to be adult.

He looks great, by the way. He was wearing those flowered jams or whatever they call them and a Mets cap, which should look ridiculous on a forty-three-year-old man, but they didn't. And that earring, this little diamond. I used to think that was the sexiest thing. His hair may be thinning a bit under the cap, but otherwise he looks terrific.

Am I rattling? Honestly, I don't know why I'm so unhinged. I run into an ex, ex-whatever, we exchange pleasantries, act civilized. The awful thing was, this is embarrassing, my heart was pattering away, I could hear it the whole time we were talking.

We're walking across the baseball diamonds, and I tell him I've moved over to a bigger agency, that I'm handling Diane Ladd and Ben Kingsley, and he's telling me about Thailand, how serene and happy the people there are, and there's this little outdoor café that I would love, it has monkeys that aren't in cages, that perch on your shoulder while you eat.

Mind you, all of this is said like we're just old friends. Not old friends, like no time has passed, like we're still the way we were. There's no allusion to our parting, my parting. How would you phrase it? He was the one who suggested ending it, so technically I suppose he left me. The fact that I did the actual leaving is beside the point.

I've never told you exactly what happened, have I? I went in originally because I was having trouble sleeping after my divorce. I won't go into the reasons behind that— suffice it to say that I got over my insomnia within the first six months and kept going because for that one hour every week I was happy.

Happy? I don't know, not euphoric certainly, but I felt more at home there than I did in my own apartment. Time stopped in that room. For fifty minutes, anyway.

His office was on the top floor of a brownstone in the West Village. You entered through a gate off the street into a courtyard, and then up four flights of stairs, very narrow and squeaky. And at the top was this wonderful garret, with a skylight and a door that opened onto a tiny iron balcony. The windows faced the back side of a convent and a garden that was maintained by the nuns.

The room was so quiet and separate from the city. In the summer months the smell of lilies and cooking floated up through the open windows. Birds nested in the ivy, pigeons, but other birds too. Sparrows.

We talked about my fears and my childhood, all the standard stuff, my trust issues, my dreams, et cetera. Not just mine, though, his as well. Douglas was never a classic analyst; he would throw in more than the occasional "How do you feel about that?" I got to know him rather well over the two years. When life was going well, we talked about fantasies. I know what you're thinking, not just sexual fantasies, fantasies about being a child again or time traveling. He told me then that he wanted to visit Thailand, that he wanted to study with the monks there. He actually did go that Easter, and then again in August. That second trip, he brought me back a picture of Hanuman, the monkey general, painted on green silk.

Mine? Well, I had one wonderful fantasy that the room we were in was actually in Rome, that the voices I sometimes heard from across the courtyard were speaking Italian, and that when I passed outside the courtyard, there would be piazzas and open plazas filled with women in black. This fantasy also included Douglas, of course, the city of love and all that. It was part of the transference process; even I had read enough Freud to recognize that. That knowledge, by the way, is no comfort. It's disorienting enough to fall in love, without the added embarrassment of knowing that your feelings are as programmed as a laboratory rat's.

Douglas and I, in my fantasy, would float through the canals in a gondola. I know the canals are in Venice, not Rome, but in my fantasy they were in Rome. He stood at the rear of the gondola, pushing us through a dark labyrinth of canals, under bridges with smiling gargoyles. Pretty transparent, tunnels and a gondola instead of a train. Probably the only original thing in the whole fantasy is that he was singing chants. Buddhist chants, I suppose. I couldn't understand the words, but the music was atonal.

I don't know. I guess the chants would be significant, the fact that I didn't understand them. I don't know.

Our last session, or rather the next to the last, I was rambling on about something, much as I'm doing now, and he was turning his pen over and over in his hand, with this look on his face. Like his dog had died. He never developed the ability to appear raptly attentive when he was not, and he's not a good liar. I would imagine this candor is a professional liability, but it was one of the things I really loved about him. His emotions were very close to the surface, almost in a feminine way. Most men, I think, seem to regard their feelings as awkward and embarrassing, like a second pair of hands.

I asked him what was the matter, was he all right? At first, he tried to evade the whole thing, asked me to please continue. I said, "Listen, I consider you a friend, and something is obviously bothering you."

Finally he said he wanted to discuss the possibility of my ending therapy, "graduating," I believe was his term. He felt I had come so far, that I was ready to move on. And he would be leaving for another vacation to Bangkok in a month, so the timing seemed apt, et cetera, et cetera. I don't remember his exact reasoning, but anyway, how would I feel about this?

I felt like all the air had been sucked out of the room. I felt much worse than when my husband, Eric, moved his things out. What I said was, ready or not, I liked being there, I liked being with him.

He said, "I like you being here, too, Abby, and I'll miss you when you go. But, frankly, I can't go on taking your money simply because we enjoy each other's company. There are ethical considerations."

I still don't buy that. I had a good settlement from Eric, and I was making not a bad living besides. If I wanted to spend it on being with him, that was certainly as valid as spending it at Sak's or going to a spa. And since when do therapists decide you don't need them anymore? Okay, I know that's the goal, but I've never heard of a person being dumped by their shrink before. You're supposed to leave them. I guess he didn't see it that way.

We spent the next session talking about closure. That was his agenda, in any case. In reality, I spent the hour making a complete ass of myself, telling him that I loved him, that I didn't give a damn whether it was transference or not. And how could he be so sure? Transference is endowing the therapist with the qualities of the ideal mother or father, right? Well, you tell me, when have you fallen in love and not done just that?

He reassured me that my feelings were natural and nothing to be ashamed of. His exact words. Nothing to be ashamed of. Which, of course, made me feel perfectly foolish and angry besides.

"I'm not the one who's ashamed of his feelings," I said. Listen, I know about countertransference. More to the point, I know love when I see it, when I've seen it. I looked in his face and it was all there.

I said, "Do me a favor, Douglas. Explain to me why only the patient has human feelings. How come I can't ask you how you're feeling and get a straight answer?"

You know what he said? He said, and I quote, "I have human feelings, Abby, but you are more important here than my feelings." And then he went on to tell me about the bodhisattvas. They're Buddhist monks, but they're teachers. And they make this sacrifice. Instead of floating off to Nirvana, they stay behind so they can help other people.

Which sounds real impressive until you ask yourself, "Do I want someone who renounces his feelings telling me how to be happy?"

We were supposed to have another couple of sessions, but suddenly I just didn't see the point. I had this moment of clarity, and I realized that there's no mileage in trying to convince someone to recognize happiness when it comes. You can talk and talk and talk and talk, and the truth gets further away. Some truths aren't gotten to through words. That's heresy in your profession, I know, and who am I to be criticizing? After all, here I am. Still blathering on. Of course, I'm not exactly happy now either.

How much time do we have left?

The cherry trees are blooming in the park now. Douglas and I walked the length of the long meadow and through this place over near the library called the Vale of Kashmir. It's pretty run-down now, broken beer bottles, et cetera, but it must have been beautiful once. The cherry trees were thick with blossoms, and every little riff of breeze snowed petals on us.

Douglas was telling me a story about a monk he met who can amplify his heartbeat. He sat in a room, in Thailand, with this monk and he listened to the pulse of the man's heart, this slow drumming swelling louder and louder. Douglas said it felt like being inside the womb, like a memory of perfect contentment.

The funny thing is I nodded and smiled, like I'd been there, like I remembered it, too. The room, the feeling of peace. Like a déjà vu or something. And then I realized it was the sound of my own heart.

CONFESSIONS OF A FALLING WOMAN

If this letter reaches you, it will have to be by some divine accident. I know you are no longer living at this address, and the phone company no longer lists you in Chicago. That doesn't surprise me; after all I was the one who loved cities, not you. All your talk, after the accident, about going back to Minot, working on your dad's farm, how you wanted to sleep in the dark again. Anyplace but North Dakota, I used to think. It might please you to know that I've come around to your way of thinking, Russ. Not geographically, but I have a small garden. A few tomato plants, some basil and mint, a row of spinach. It's not ambitious, but things grow in it.

In fact, I took a shot and called Information in Minot. I also tried to get in touch with you through Audie, and I'm sorry to hear of his passing. He was a sweet man, and he treated me like a daughter, even after the divorce.

So my only hope, absurd perhaps, is that you've left a for-
warding address and the postal service will find you for me.

You must be wondering why I am trying to contact
you now, after all this time. Perhaps it will strike you as a
thoughtless invasion of your privacy, or worse, a deliberate
unkindness, an attempt to open up old wounds.

Another possibility occurs to me: that you have put our
life behind you entirely, and I will have to rely on idle curiosity. I'm trying to imagine you now, wherever you are, holding this letter in your hands and glancing over the lines, like
a plea from some charity. What does she want from me?

Here it is: I want you to hear me out. An apology is a
limp thing, I know that, and it's late by about eleven years,
but here it is.

Do you remember the night in the hospital, we were in
the waiting room, and you said you had noticed the tires on
the Chevy the week before, that they were a little bald? It
was just something you muttered, you probably don't remember. You were saying a lot of things, and your hair was
coming out in handfuls, little tufts of hair coming off in my
hands when I stroked your head. The medic said it was
shock. Still, you might have noticed that I didn't shush you,
that I didn't say "No, honey, it's not your fault."

The brakes had locked, and I realize now that new tires
wouldn't have made any difference. But at the time, I heard
an explanation in your words. Our child couldn't die unless
someone had been irresponsible, I thought, unless someone

was to blame. I don't remember much else of that year, except being tired. It took so much effort to keep that image of balding tires at bay, to keep on loving you, to keep silent when I wanted to scream. Listening to you talk about moving to Minot, as if the city were at fault. And then when you came home from work with the name of a counselor, a grief counselor, as though we required instruction on grieving. You said we had to come to terms with Megan's death before we could go on. What you didn't know, of course, was that I had already found a way. God knows, I didn't want to blame you, but the alternative was unthinkable, random horror. Forget what I told you when I left, that you didn't meet my needs, that I needed my space, or whatever was the current jargon. I traded you in for the illusion that the world still made sense.

I didn't know it then, that you can let go and still live. There's a story I heard recently, a parable about a man who falls off a cliff. As he's falling he grabs onto a branch or a root sticking out from the cliff. He hangs on for dear life, clutching that thin twig, but he's not strong enough and his grip is slipping, and finally his fingers slip loose. And he falls . . . six inches. I clung to that image of balding tires for almost a decade. For what it's worth, I want you to know that I've finally let go.

About seven months ago, I was pushing a cart down the cereal aisle at the Grand Union. (You may have noticed the postmark; I bought a small house in Croton a few years ago.

It's an hour to New York, the best of both worlds.) You know how they play Muzak in the supermarkets? I was pushing the cart, and this song exploded in my head, very loud. It was Tina Turner singing "What's Love Got to Do with It?" Except it was inside my head, like picking up a radio station in a gold filling. I just stood there, terrified, gripping the handle of the cart, listening to Tina blaring in my brain. And then it stopped, she clicked off. I looked around to see if anyone else had heard it. A woman in a pink sweat suit picked a box of All-Bran off a shelf and glanced over the print on the side of the carton.

That was the first time; it happened again. Of course, I didn't tell anyone, not even the man I'm seeing. Peter is a good man, and he has since surprised me with his reserve of humor, but our relationship was not yet intimate enough to admit insanity. You see, I also smelled burning rubber sometimes. That was what made me think it was a sign: the stench of tires burning. At the time, I was sure that God or my psyche was trying to tell me something. Something to do with Megan or with you.

I made a list of the songs and the times when I had heard them. The rush-hour train home, between Dobbs Ferry and Tarrytown: Beethoven's *Pastoral* Symphony. While taking my dinner out of the microwave: Dean Martin singing "White Christmas." In the shower: "Something's Coming," from *West Side Story*. I bought the tapes and listened to them at night, over and over again, trying to decode their meaning. Tina Turner was telling me that love was a secondhand emotion, but Dean Martin suggested that the memory of family and home are the things that sustain you through loneliness. Maybe the message had something to do with treetops glistening, a pastoral scene, but that discounted *West Side Story*. "Something's coming, something good." I tried anagrams. Finally, I went to an analyst for help. He sent me to an MD, who sent me to a specialist. As it turns out, I have a brain tumor.

I've been told that as a tumor grows it presses against the brain tissue and sometimes things misfire. The songs I heard were random bytes lodged in my brain, not even favorite songs. The smell of burning rubber is a common symptom, by the way, if I had known what I was looking for. Perfectly logical, but there is no meaning attached to any of it.

Are you still with me, Russ?

There's no logic to a brain tumor, to a car spinning out on a few wet leaves. It doesn't make sense to die. Not at five, not at forty-three or -four, not even, I suppose, at ninety. It's very hard not to take it personally. Not to think God's out to get me, to punish me for something. But for what, Russ? Living?

And everything else that has happened to me—you, Megan, Peter, my entire life—it doesn't form some grand pattern. Not one that I can recognize, anyway. It seems so ridiculous now that I could have blamed you for Meggie, for our unhappiness afterward. There is no one to blame this time around. I can't tell you what a relief that is, finally.

I don't hear music anymore. They removed the tumor, although there are still bad cells brewing in there, despite a first round of chemo. I suppose the odds are against me, but then I don't believe in odds anymore. I believe it could just as easily go my way as not.

You should see me, Russ. I'm learning to do quite stylish things with scarves. I look at my face in the mirror and don't recognize it; however, I do look vaguely like Georgia O'Keeffe, which pleases me. My eyes look stronger than they did when I was well, and the bones in my face have come out like a landscape. All the fat has been carved away. Please don't misunderstand me here. I'm not reappearing in your life with any ulterior motives. I expect and hope that you have remarried; I can't imagine you alone. And to be honest, I can't afford a regret that huge. It seems like a form of suicide to regret any part of my life, even the mistakes, and suicide, at this stage of the game, seems like gilding the lily. Redundant, anyway. Still, I imagine different sequences. It's like a parlor game. I back up a few moves and try to see how else I might have played this, what other lives were open to me. I imagine the possibilities, the maze of random choices. And I always come back to you. It doesn't change a thing, but I think it's important to say.

I never told you this, in the morning it had seemed too silly to talk about. Remember that first summer after Megan was born, when we went out to North Dakota to show Audie his new granddaughter? There was a night I couldn't sleep.

The bed in your old room was too narrow for both of us. So I sneaked downstairs, threw your coat on over my nightgown and went outside. I started walking down the road from the house out toward the main road. There was no moon, no neighboring lights, nothing but an icy dust of stars from one edge of the earth to the other. At some point, I saw a slow beam of headlights in the distance, tracing a line across the dark, as straight and steady as a satellite. I walked toward it for what must have been a long time, although neither of us seemed to change position.

I had no sense of how far I'd gone, until after I turned around and started to head back. The sodium vapor light on the side of Audie's barn glowed like a firefly. I suddenly felt dizzy—the enormity of black space, the emptiness of the planet. You and our daughter slept inside that tiny light, and our three lives seemed in that moment so tenuously connected, like a miraculous accident of crossed paths. I was too frightened to sleep when I returned. I felt like someone who had been visited by angels, struck dumb by the sight of terrifying beauty. You said the next morning I looked haunted, and I told you I'd had bad dreams.

You see why I couldn't go back there after she died.

What I keep coming back to, Russ, is that you and Megan were a mystery in my life. I expected to marry a businessman, my father more or less, to raise two anonymous children, to vacation in Europe once or twice, to live out my days unsurprised. God knows, I never suspected I would care for a man who was afraid to fly, who liked canned peas and couldn't be trusted not to say whatever came into his head. I never imagined I would be wrenched with love for a child who had your temper, my crooked teeth, and a laugh that neither of us had ever heard before. Where did that laugh come from? Even if Megan had lived, she would have remained a mystery. Even if I had stayed, I would never have been able to explain the fact of you in my life. Just pure dumb luck.

I feel inexplicably lucky. Against all reason, I believe that I can send these words out into the night and they will find you. You needn't write back. If you hear me, that's more than enough.

DAN IN THE GRAY FLANNEL RAT SUIT

If I were to go to sleep right this minute, I could get maybe four hours. But that's a long shot. An inversion seems to be taking place in my life: I float blearily through days that are fleeting as dreams, and then snap to at about midnight for what feels like my real life.

What I'm discovering is that the life of an insomniac very probably resembles that of a cloistered monk. Take away the unexpected diversions that fill up one's days, the soothing distraction of other human beings, and then just try to avoid becoming contemplative. The mysteries of the universe saturate the night air, questions hang unanswered in the silence. The trick here is to stay anchored to the planet. It is why I tend so carefully to my habits.

Midnight, I walk the dog. Then I slide into bed beside my wife, Robin, and go through the motions of trying to sleep. I shift into a series of positions: on my side with a pillow tucked between my knees, then on my back, my stomach, and so on, eventually returning to the fetal position. After a half dozen or so reps, it's up to check that the front door and windows are locked. They are. Back to bed. Next, a review of every relaxation exercise I can remember from years of acting classes. Somewhere in there, Puck usually has to be walked again. He is twelve years old, and the heart medication the vet has him on causes a prodigious thirst. Once I've escorted him down to the street and back, we both get a drink of water, he gets a dog biscuit, and I help myself to a few cookies. Then I settle in front of the tube and run the channels. Sometimes I get lucky and stumble onto a good movie. One of the channels is doing a Gene Kelly festival this week, so I watched the last half of *On the Town* before I came to bed tonight. After a while, I undress again and return to bed. I lie in the dark, as I'm doing now, watching for the shadows in the room to shift, waiting for the dark to gather itself into some recognizably malevolent shape.

The street lamps cast a dim light through the window shades, enough to see bulky shadows in the bedroom: the highboy, the television, the valet stand lurking in the corner. Now and then a car swishes by up on Prospect Park Drive. Farther out, past our quiet neighborhood, the city buzzes with sirens and car alarms and the muted rumble of traffic on the BQE, but my ears are tuned to this room, the rooms on either side, the circumscribed territory of a city dweller.

All is quiet just now, except for the rhythm of Robin's breath and the dog's light snores, as muted as the sounds of the sea in a shell.

Four weeks ago, a man broke into our apartment. We had rented a video, ordered in Chinese, and were holed up in the bedroom, stripped to the skin because the night was sweltering and this is the only room with AC. A Thursday night, every light in the place on, the television murmuring, the ancient air conditioner rattling. No one who wasn't high as a kite would even think about breaking into an apartment when people were obviously inside. It's partly the irrationality of the whole incident that keeps me awake. In New York, you operate on the principle that while, yes, there's a lot of evil in the city, it's more or less predictable. Not like the suburbs, where the violence is hidden and explodes randomly, where the killers all look like computer programmers. Here, there are rules. You put dead bolts on the doors and gates on the windows, you assume the "don't fuck with me" expression when you're on the street, you avoid certain neighborhoods, certain parks, you keep to the front cars on the subway, you spring for a cab if it's late. And when you read about some tourist who got pushed onto the train tracks or a woman who was beaten in the park, you remind yourself that *you* don't stand at the front edge of the subway platform. *You* wouldn't dream of going jogging in the park before dawn. It's a terrible tragedy, of course, but they broke the rules.

I go over it in my head frame by frame, trying to figure what I've missed. The film we'd rented was a Bergman; Robin had thought maybe it would seem cooler if we were watching people shivering in bleak, snowy landscapes. Somewhere midway through, she had fallen asleep, lulled into a stupor by the drone of Swedish voices. Her freckled limbs were sprawled luxuriantly across the mattress, her hair curling in damp tendrils around her face. I can remember considering and then discarding the impulse to wake her up again. Instead, I picked at the last of the sesame noodles and was trying to see the film through to the end, when I thought I heard something in the kitchen. I pulled on my boxers and went into the kitchen. The security gate across the window was ajar.

Afterward, the cops said we should have had the window closed. Never mind that there was a locked gate covering it. Never mind that a ten-year-old couldn't squeeze his hand through the openings. According to them, I should have known that some crackhead with an hour to spare, a metal file, and the manual dexterity of Houdini could crouch on a fourth-floor fire escape and somehow saw off the lock.

There was a rustling sound coming from the study across the hall. I went into the room. A rickety thin man stood in the shadow of the open closet door, his hands pushing through the rack of winter clothes stored there. He saw me, and we stood there a long moment, eyeing each other, neither of us certain what to do next. In the dark, his eyes were glazed and bright.

I began to talk quietly, soothingly. "Everything's going to be okay. It's going to be fine. Really." Over and over, the same words, as monotonous and meaningless as the Swedish floating in from the next room.

In slow motion, his hand went into the pocket of his jacket.

"I got a gun," he said, but his hand stayed in his pocket and it was dark. It might be a gun, it might be just his hand, no way of knowing. "Turn around. Get down on your knees, motherfucker."

"I can't do that," I said, "but it's going to be all right. No one's going to get hurt."

I could hear my heart thudding in my ears and the sound of this voice, my voice, but far away and as calm and detached as a doctor's. "Everything's going to be fine. Just go back out the way you came and everything will be fine."

Miraculously, he moved to follow my instructions. I stepped away from the door, and he stepped toward it. We circumscribed a slow half-circle, like dance partners. A step, another step, the murmuring of my voice, my heart doing the rumba, and this guy, his eyes locked onto mine. He was afraid, too. I could see it.

When he got to the door, he tried to pull it shut with me inside, but my hand caught the other side of the knob and pulled back.

"It's going to be okay," my voice said. "I can't stay in here, but it's going to be okay." I thought of Robin asleep in the bedroom. Maybe a minute passed, each of us pulling, then I felt the pressure release on the other side, and the door swung open. He was disappearing into the kitchen. I followed him around the corner, still talking, and planted myself in the doorway while he backed slowly toward the open window. Under the lights of the kitchen, he looked frail and less dangerous than I'd imagined. Maybe it was the baseball cap. I remember being surprised by that, the Mets cap. I was a Mets fan, too. He was still backing up, feeling his way behind him with the hand that supposedly had held a gun. A few inches short of our goal, almost home free, he stopped, and I saw his eyes light on a paring knife in the dish rack. He grabbed it and came lunging back across the kitchen toward me. I held up my hands to block him, thinking to myself *I'm history now* and feeling remarkably calm about that. Then, for no reason that I can imagine, he stopped, the knife a bare inch from my hands, wavering, glinting. Our eyes locked again and we stood frozen like actors in a film when someone stops the projector. This is it. See, this moment, right here. This is when everything changes.

And then the film jerked to life again.

"Don't tell him I was here, man," he said, shaking the knife at me for emphasis. He backed toward the window.

"I won't."

And he scrabbled out the window and disappeared.

I stared at the open window, a minute, maybe less, before I ran into the bedroom. Robin was gone. Bedsheets were strewn across the empty mattress. I yelled her name and heard a rustling coming from under the bed. As I came around to her side, she managed to pull herself free from under the low bed frame. Her eyes were wild with terror.

"Are you all right? Robin, are you all right?" I know I wasn't thinking clearly because I had the frenzied idea that somehow he had gotten to her while I was inside the study. She shook her head and tears brimmed up in her eyes.

"I thought he had a gun." She sprang into my arms and we held each other. She was shaking, as though she had caught a chill, and foolishly I wrapped the comforter around her.

"It's all right, sweetie. He's gone. It's all over."

Now that we were safe, the fear I hadn't felt earlier bubbled up in my veins, light as helium. We might have been killed. But no, I reminded myself, Robin had been safe. She'd been hiding. And then my brain snagged on a question.

"Robin, did you call 911?"

She shook her head no, her breath coming in hiccuping sobs now. I noted the phone on the nightstand, still in its cradle.

"It's okay, sweetheart," I told her. "Everything is going to be okay now."

I was wrong about that, though. For starters, this incident has destroyed my sleep, not something I was great at to begin with. Even Robin, who can sleep like the dead for nine, ten hours at a stretch, starts at the slightest sound. She happens to be out at the moment, but it is a restless business: she jerks and twitches and occasionally whimpers something indecipherable.

Me, I watch and listen. It gives me a lot of time to think. And what I've been mulling over during these vigils is the possibility that my life has jumped the tracks. Or worse, that there were never any tracks to begin with.

Maybe a crack-addled brain can explain singling out a secure and well-lit apartment to burgle. But then, how to explain why I'm not dead, or at the very least lying in St. Vincent's recovering from multiple slash wounds and sipping my dinner through a straw? Everyone says we were lucky, no one was hurt, nothing was stolen. And maybe I should feel grateful, but it's a disconcerting thought when you get right down to it. Luck cuts both ways.

Case in point: my life as an actor. When I moved here from Tulsa in '75, I gave myself five years to make it. I wanted to be a star, but one who did interesting, offbeat work, one who, even when LA came courting, would never completely abandon his roots in the theater. The actor's actor: a De Niro, a Pacino. I never owned up to wanting the stardom part, though. Instead, I made it known that I simply wanted to do good work, to be an artist, to have a life in the theater. At the time, these seemed like humble aspirations.

Nearing the end of my fifth year in New York, my résumé listed a mercifully unnoticed workshop production, Nick in *Who's Afraid of Virginia Woolf?* at the Passaic Playhouse, the role of Flight Engineer on a TV movie of the week, and a smattering of extra work. Nights, I did phone solicitation, trying to sell vacation packages. In short, I hadn't made it by anyone's definition, but by the standards of a business where the unemployment rate hovers around ninety-two percent, I was holding my own. I had acquired my union cards and a decent, though not powerful, agent. I was paying my dues and honing my craft—*quack, quack, quack, quack, quack*—all the things I told myself while I dialed for dollars.

Then I got cast in an off-Broadway play called *Crosshairs*. I was convinced, along with the rest of the company, that we had our hands on a brilliant play, so I was not surprised, much less grateful, when the *Times* agreed. Frank Rich said my performance was "disarming" and "hilarious," and I thought that, well, yes, that was about right.

The upshot was that my life was transformed. Suddenly casting directors were chummy, women brazenly available. The show moved across town to Broadway and started raking it in. I spent money like water, picking up checks for all my unemployed friends, buying a share in a summer rental out in Montauk. I signed autographs at the stage door and pretended modest surprise when people recognized me. More important, I started getting seen regularly for film roles, and there were a few key names in the business—what's the point of dropping names now?—they liked me and were introducing me around. The end of my fifth year came and went, and if I noticed, I don't remember.

Another nine years later, I am thirty-seven years old and I don't work much in the theater anymore. No, let's be honest: I haven't done a play in three years, and months go by between auditions. I have no explanation for any of this, none whatsoever. Except luck.

When people ask what I do, I say I'm an actor. Strictly speaking, though, what I do is bartend. I still snag the occasional commercial, and every once in a while my friend Stuart throws me a job recording a book on tape, but who's kidding who? Last week, I spent a morning pretending to be a crazed rodent in hopes of landing a national for Dobbin Copiers. I had no lines, just reaction shots: curious, excited, hysterical. Facial expressions were out, because there is some kind of mask involved. "It's all in the squeaks, the body language," the director told me with that amplified earnestness that commercial people indulge in to convince themselves they're doing something meaningful. I found myself thinking, as I squeaked and squealed for all I was worth, so this is what it comes to.

Everything could change again tomorrow—that's what keeps you in the game—but eventually you also have to face the possibility that it might not.

Down on the street, a car alarm shrieks to life. Robin's breathing suspends, her eyes snap open. We listen, wait through the moments it might take for the owner to stumble from his bed and into the street, but no one comes. The alarm caterwauls and then changes key to a series of bleats. I get up, peer out the window, see nothing, pull the window closed, and turn the AC on high to muffle the keening howls.

"Have you ever been to Santa Fe?" She doesn't look at me when she asks.

"No."

"We went there once, to look at a horse Dad was thinking about buying. I remember I was surprised at how cold it was; it was December, but I thought everywhere in the Southwest was like Phoenix. It started to snow. and the arroyos blurred and turned white. It was the quietest place in the whole world."

"Sounds nice," I say, guardedly.

The morning after the break-in, Robin announced that she wanted to leave New York. A pretty natural sentiment, given the events of the previous night, but not the kind of comment you want to give too much weight. There's a garbage strike, one too many snowstorms in February, whatever, and everyone talks about getting out. I figured that Robin's was just one of those empty threats that every New Yorker makes against the city.

But she's still circling the subject. She reads the travel section first on Sundays now. She cooks up all sorts of possibilities in places like Durham, North Carolina, or Missoula, Montana. Every night it's a different town, and she puts herself back to sleep dreaming about the cottage or houseboat or cabin we would live in, the vegetables she would plant in our garden.

"If we were willing to go out a bit, we could still afford to get a place with a little land," she continues.

"What would we do in Santa Fe?" I ask.

"I don't know, exactly." Her voice stiffens. "We'd come up with something, though. We're bright, capable people." What she doesn't say, though, and it hangs heavy in the air between us, is that her options are greater than mine. She can get a personnel job anywhere, but I can't imagine there's much demand for actors in Santa Fe.

"I just can't see myself there," I tell her.

"Well, where can you see yourself?"

"I don't know."

She sighs, deeply frustrated with me.

"Honestly," I say, "don't you think the idea of packing up the jalopy and heading out West is a little over the top?" Sometimes a note of levity works with Robin. I'm guessing from her silence that this isn't one of those times. I try a different tack. "After all," I remind her soothingly, "this is our home."

Robin's eyes drift to the windows, to the streetlight seeping through the metal security gates and making hatch-marked shadows on the window shades.

"You yourself said that you might as well be in Kansas," she says.

"Well, for Christ's sake, I didn't mean it literally."

No matter how innocuously we begin, every discussion these days circles round to some question of our future, just as it did eleven years ago when we were still trying to determine whether this unlikely pairing was actually going to work. Now, it would seem, everything we agreed on is up for review again.

Maybe this upcoming trip will help. Wednesday morning, we're flying up to Maine to visit my father-in-law, who has a summer home on Penobscot Bay. Six days cooped up with Jack Casterline and his loony tunes wife is not my idea of a vacation, but I can't really kick since Jack is footing the bill.

The window shades are fading to gray with the first light. It occurs to me that I haven't actually witnessed the sun rise or set since I can't remember when, this despite the fact that I'm awake during most of them these days. There is no horizon in New York, no line dividing sky and earth. Even during the day, the sun is felt more than seen, the heat of it seeping down between the long shadows in midtown and wavering back up from the concrete. Shards of sunlight refract off glass buildings, but the sun itself, the sky . . .

I wish I could follow Robin into her dreams. I wish I could turn my back on my life and pull up the covers and be in a snowy arroyo somewhere.

But I have promises to keep. And miles to go before I sleep. And yada yada yada.

*   *   *

I'm on the lookout for signs and portents these days, and what I'm discovering is that if one is looking, they appear in multitudes. Even the most daily event sprouts wings, becomes vastly significant. I'm on my way to this audition, and halfway between my building and the subway, the summer sky suddenly darkens to a septic green and splits open. The water is starting to drip off my chin, and just as I'm warming into a long string of curses, an empty cab materializes out of the rain like a messenger from heaven. I hail the cab over to the curb, slide into the backseat, give the turbaned driver the address, then settle back and close my eyes for a few minutes. When I open them, we are inexplicably heading up Sixth Avenue and a good thirty blocks north of my destination. It turns out the cabbie doesn't speak English; he responds to each of my frenzied corrections with an uncomprehending nod. The winds shift again, we turn south, the meter ticks over into four digits, and it occurs to me that this is the difficulty with trying to read your own life: from the center, each sign seems to radiate out in a different direction.

We have just crossed Canal again, and he is heading doggedly back uptown. I check my watch: it is 9:20. If I cut my losses and get out here, I could still make it on foot. I rap on the Plexiglas and signal the cabbie to pull over.

When he flips up the meter and his eyes meet mine in the rearview mirror, he smiles cautiously, expectant. Against all odds, he seems to believe that a miracle has deposited us at the mysterious address I've been yammering from the back-seat. A few minutes ago, I might have argued the fare with the guy. Now I see my own bewildered self reflected in his smooth face. I stuff fourteen dollars into the slot and climb out into the downpour.

I am losing my grip.

The audition is for a new play by Arthur Haines at Tribeca Rep. I'm reading for Hal, this right-wing preacher who's running for a Senate seat somewhere out of the Midwest. It's not the lead, the play's actually about the gay speechwriter who's working on his campaign, but Hal is an interesting character with some good scenes. And it's eight, ten weeks of work, a good play, guaranteed press. Not that I'm in a position to be choosy.

Three blocks from the theater I slow to a fast walk and start running lines in my head.

"What are they saying about us in the *Herald*, Terry?"

(Blah, blah, blah, blah)

"Well, Paul tells us we'll be persecuted for our faith."

(Blah, blah, blah)

I duck and weave through a phalanx of umbrellas at the corner, check for traffic, dive across the intersection.

"I'm not asking you to agree with me privately, Terry."

(Blah, blah)

"Don't take advantage of my good manners."

My guess is that a lot of actors are going in there and reading Hal as a cardboard villain or a buffoon, which is a mistake. This guy's likable and sincere and convincing. That's what gives the play its tension.

In the elevator, I peel away my suit jacket and shake water off myself like a spaniel. I get up to the offices, sign in: name, agency, union membership. I'm on time, which turns out to be irrelevant. They're running behind—the small reception area is clogged with nervous Hals and Terrys. A half-dozen actors are bent intently over copies of the script or staring into some private distance. Two guys in the far corner are shooting the breeze, ostentatiously at ease. One of them is Brad Whalen, who works here all the time. He's not right for Hal, but then again, you never know. I'm hoping he just dropped by.

The other guy is Kyle McCann. We have the same agent. It's not just jealousy when I say the guy is a bimbo, completely without talent and maddeningly successful. At the moment, he is lounging against the wall in the studied pose of a jeans ad and casually tapping a rolled-up script against the brick.

"When'd you get back, man?" Although the question is addressed to Brad, Kyle pitches his volume just enough so all of us can listen in.

"Last week. I took a couple extra days after we were done shooting and went on down to the Keys. You ever been there?"

"No. I did a show at the Burt Reynolds with Nate Bellogi. We kept talking about going down there, fishing some marlin. But you know how it is with Nate." You listening up, fans? He's pals with Nate Bellogi. Nate, not Nathan as he's known to the great unwashed. "Monday would roll around and I'd just drag myself out to the nearest beach and sleep it off."

"I'm telling you, Kyle, you gotta go."

I borrow the men's room key and head back out the door. In the bathroom, I check the mirror: under the fluorescent light, I look dull-eyed and pasty, like something washed up on Kyle's beach. My hair is slicked to my scalp from the rain; below the line of my jacket, my pants are water-stained and sticky with the damp heat. I spindle a couple feet of paper towel off the roll and mop water out of my hair, off my face. Then I run a comb through my hair, take a leak, wash my hands, and glance over the sides again. I say a few lines into the mirror, trying to recall what I did last night when I ran the lines with Robin. My voice sounds as phony in my ears as the jackass back in the waiting room. Whatever confidence I had about this audition, I must have left behind in the cab.

This is the first legit job I've gone out for since March. It's summer and things are dead all over town. Still, last month I dropped by my agent's office with some flimsy excuse (in the neighborhood, heard they're casting such and such, went to school with the director) just to remind him I was still alive. For better or worse, Zak is probably too nice for this business: he didn't tell his receptionist to get rid of me. Instead, he sat me down and lectured me about taking a vacation, for

God's sake, giving him a break and going somewhere nice. He recommended Block Island, "but don't eat before you get on the ferry."

I'd be better off with one of those anorexic killers who live on coffee and hardball contract negotiations and bitter gossip, but I've stuck with Zak because, frankly, I get enough rejection in this business without taking it from my agent. I wouldn't go so far as to describe us as close, but we get a kick out of each other, and we've continued to stick it out when there were smarter options on both sides. There are marriages based on less. It'd be a good thing to get this job, if for no other reason than to justify his faith.

I run the lines until they stop echoing back in my ears, then head back into the office and return the key. Brad Whalen and Kyle are gone. I scout a chair next to a husky blond fellow who's carrying on an animated but soundless conversation with himself. His eyebrows raise then furrow, his lips move, then his features twist into an exaggerated expression of disdain. It's like watching a silent movie.

My name is called and I startle. I pull myself to my feet, take a deep breath, begin smiling inside my head. I don the persona of Hal: confident, earnest. I get ready to do my stuff.

Bippety bip bippety bop, I'm in the door, all smiles and bonhomie. The wax museum is lined up behind a long table: the director, the playwright, the casting director, the assistant to the director, each one sporting the glazed facsimile of a smile. I do the lightning round of introductions, shake hands up and down the table like a seasoned politician, go to the empty stool in front of the table, and ask the reader her name, which I promptly forget. Then the scene. It flies, they're awake, and they're asking to see something else, the scene with the reporter. I slide into gear again, and then it happens: I step through the looking glass. On the other side, there is a reporter asking me questions about a young woman Hal knew in Grand Rapids. Katherine Sellers. Kathy. She was wearing a white nightgown that held the shadows of her thighs, and her shoulders were like small birds. Just that once, late at night, while Janice and the children slept upstairs. When she moved underneath me, I heard wings rustling. It might have been a dream. A brilliant light shines directly in my eyes and faces swim feverishly at the edges of my vision. I smile into the light, willing myself to speak slowly into the proffered microphone. "Miss Sellers lived with our family briefly while she was attending college. She helped my wife, Janice, with the boys after Kirk was born. Miss Sellers attended our church and was a fine young Christian woman. I don't know why she would fabricate this kind of . . ." I feel like I'm going to puke. Some cold and predatory corner of my brain, though, is measuring the auditioners, gauging the heat of their attention. They have stepped across with me.

When the scene is over, there is a fraction of a minute before the tension snaps and we're back in the room. The

DEBRA DEAN

playwright, Arthur Haines, grins confidentially to me. "That was great, Dan," as though we've known each other for years. The director nods his agreement and seems to be looking me over again, envisioning me in the role. There's a brief whispered exchange, then the casting director says, "Good reading, Dan. Thanks." I'm out the door. Ten minutes, tops. That's all it takes to change the direction your life is heading in.

It has stopped raining, but the air is still steamy and tropical with the smells of overripe garbage and fruit. Sun glints off water coursing down the flooded street. Like Gene Kelly, I want to stamp through the gutters, dance into those puddles, to hell with my already soggy loafers. Instead, I wait expectantly at the curb, careful not to get splashed, bouncing on my twinkle toes and waiting for the sea of traffic to part just long enough for me to dart across. I'm giddy, ready for my luck to change.

As it turns out, I didn't have to wait long. Good news was already blinking on my answering machine by the time I walked in the door this afternoon. Beep: Tribeca Rep wants to see me again in the morning. And in a when-it-rains-it-pours mode, another beep: I've been put on first refusal for the Dobbins Copier commercial. Beep, beep, beep, beep, beep.

It's premature to start counting my chickens. I know that from experience. A callback is a long way from an offer. And

156

even a first refusal doesn't necessarily mean they'll use you. They're covering their asses. These days, there may be two or three other actors on the back burner with you.

Still, I can't stop my brain from racing on ahead without me, whizzing down the arterials, turning out at every promising side street. Part of me may be standing here at my post behind the bar, but the rest is far away, lofted into a future from which I can see this restaurant—the speckled pink walls, the framed and autographed photo of Sinatra over the cash register, the same tapes looping over and over, and even myself, the bartender zesting lemons like a zombie—all of it tinted with nostalgia.

At nine o'clock, there are three customers on the other side of the bar, a pair of nurses and, of course, Marv. Marv is the professional hazard of this job, the regular who monopolizes the TV and takes all his phone calls at the bar, dispenses unwanted advice, and generally makes himself at home. I'm his "old buddy," a dubious status accorded to anyone pouring out the CC and soda, and carrying with it the burden of hearing whatever thoughts are currently circulating through his sodden brain. Right now, he's holding forth on some theory he's heard concerning bats, the depletion of the bat population. It seems to have something to do with architecture and Vatican II; I've been tuning in only just often enough to nod in the right places, so I may have lost a critical thread. On the floor, it is similarly quiet, only a few couples becalmed on a sea of white tables. The ceiling fans tick lethargically, pushing dust motes through the warm air. The waiters shift from one foot to the other, scoping out their tables on the sly and then slipping out to the kitchen for a smoke. A typical Monday night, the dead shift in the week. I'm only half here, but that's more than enough.

"They slept under the eaves and in the bell tower. All those doodads served a purpose, is what he's saying, you know?" Yes, we must still be on bats.

"If you want to have bats, you gotta have belfries," I joke.

"Well, that's not exactly the point." Marv waves it away impatiently. "You don't want to get hung up on the bats per se. It's what's behind the thing."

"I see." I have no idea what the point is, but I pretend to give it my fullest consideration.

"It's a whatchamacallit. *You* know," he accuses, "when you say one thing but you really mean something else?"

"I don't know—a lie?"

Marv appraises me slowly, working his chin from side to side.

"You being a smart-ass or just stupid?"

His mood can flip on a dime, even in mid-sentence, and you never know what will trip the switch. Most nights, I refill his drink on the fly, making sure not to pause too long near his stool, in a pinch escaping my cage with some feigned need to restock something or other. But tonight my expansiveness extends even to Marv. So what if he insists, ridiculously, on acting the part of the neighborhood don? I feel something akin to the affection one has for the recently dead—that old dog Marvin with his scuffed white loafers and his half-baked stories about what a truly decent fellow Rocky Graziano was or the time he and Dean Martin and a bunch of the guys drove up from Atlantic City at four in the morning for corned beef sandwiches. What a character. I pour him a healthy shot on the house, and we're buddies again.

I might actually get out of here for good. Why not? The way I've got it figured, the folks at Tribeca must have put the call in to Zak before I was even out of the building. I'm perfect for the part and they knew it, didn't even wait until the end of the day to weigh their options. And they're hot. They've moved something uptown every year for the past three seasons. So, let's say the play does well, pulls in some good reviews; there's no reason it couldn't be a contender. It could move to Broadway, and I could be looking at a long-term gig.

Then there's the commercial. It's not art, it's not even acting, but it's money. Maybe even serious money. The session fee for an on-camera principal is about five hundred, but the real money is in the residuals. Depending on how long it runs and in what markets, a national commercial can snag you ten grand before it plays out. One I did five years ago still brings in a nice little chunk of change every thirteen weeks; in fact, a large percentage of the money I've made in my career can be traced directly to one day spent reaching over and over again into an ice chest and pulling out a couple of beers.

The two waiters are huddled at the service end of the bar, engaged in their own forecasting. Beneath Marv's raspy drone, I hear Yusef grimly predict that they'll be lucky to go home with forty dollars apiece tonight.

Carrie takes the pluckier view, that we still might get a late-night rush after the concert. The Philharmonic is playing up in the park, and she's pinning her hopes on a mob of hungry Schubert lovers storming Picardi's.

"Maybe people would come in to drink but not for dinner," Yusef pronounces, shaking his head stubbornly. "This is it."

"I'm just saying a couple of tables." Carrie turns to me for confirmation, bright and flirty. "What do you think?"

"One way or the other, makes no difference to me."

She smirks. "Well, what's gotten into you?"

"Oh, nothing much. I had a good day is all."

Under this Gary Cooperish reticence, I'm actually itching to tell someone. I haven't even filled in Robin yet, though this is simply a matter of our paths not having crossed since this morning. Only a habitual superstition against jinxing my good fortune keeps me quiet now. I don't want to end up like one of those sad cases who's always blathering about some deal in the pipeline. Better to take everyone by surprise, walk in here one night and spring it on them. Sorry, my friends, it's been nice knowing you. Hasta la vista. Farewell.

Just as Yusef predicted, we wind down the evening nearly as poor as we started it. Before he leaves, Marv makes a point of discreetly palming a five-dollar bill to me, as though I might be embarrassed to publicly accept a tip. I lock up and am home just after eleven, eager to share my news. I come through the door calling out to Robin, who emerges from the study, her arms heaped with folded clothes. She swipes a distracted kiss past my cheek as she passes into the bedroom, her voice trailing behind.

"How was work?"

"It sucked. Now ask me if I care."

I wait, the proverbial cat that ate the canary. But she doesn't pick up her cue, so I blunder through a garbled replay of my day. I'm on first refusal for the rodent thing. It's shooting Friday. And, ta-dah, I've got a callback with Tribeca Rep. Arthur Haines was impressed—you should've seen. I'm not saying I've got it (knock on wood), but I gave the best audition of my life. It just sang, the whole damn thing. And if I get the commercial, we could be talking some serious money in the bank.

There is a long pause after I wind down. When she speaks, her voice is precise and even, as though she were balancing something on its edge.

"So you haven't actually booked the commercial, right?"

"Not yet."

"You've just agreed to be on call this Friday."

"Right."

Her blue eyes ice over with disdain. "Congratulations."

It occurs to me that I'm missing something here. For some inexplicable reason, she is intentionally trying to puncture my good mood. It's not like I have that many great days to string together. Today was one. Then it hits me. I'm supposed to be in Maine on Friday.

"If you're upset about the trip"—I'm still not sure this is the problem—"okay, I blew it. I should have consulted you first. I'm sorry."

Robin remains silent and impassive. If I thought I was going to get off that easy, I'm about to be disappointed. Not a chance, bub.

"Listen, they're going to be up there all summer. Can't we just postpone it a few days?"

"I can't just pick up and go anytime, Dan." She pauses while we both add the silent coda that, unlike me, she has a real job, the kind that pays a grown-up salary and benefits in exchange for her freedom.

"Besides, that's not the point," she says. "You've been broody and miserable for I don't know how long. Skulking around the house, making me feel guilty if I'm not miserable, too. Then you start hinting around about burning your union cards, calling up Zak and throwing in the towel, and I fall for it. You really had me going this time. I'm thinking, well, maybe this is a good thing. You know, hard but good. Maybe we can start planning a life. But we can't even plan a vacation."

Contrition fails me. "You call that a vacation? Spending a week with Jack and Mina?"

Robin draws herself up into the rigidly correct posture she assumes when she is furious. "All that matters to you is that a bunch of people you don't even know like you. You're like Sally Field. It's pathetic. You get a couple of auditions and, presto, everything else vanishes. You're right back in it. I don't matter. Nothing else matters but waiting for the damn phone to ring."

"Well, shit, I'm sorry to louse up your plans. I was just under the impression we could use the money."

"Money has nothing to do with this."

"What the hell am I doing this for, then? Because I thought it was the money. So what is it? You tell me. The thrill of dressing up in a rat costume?"

"I don't know why you're doing this. But don't pretend it's for us."

Robin gets up, stalks over to the old desk in the corner, and begins yanking open drawers and rifling through the contents. She pulls out an opened pack of Marlboro Lights and continues searching the drawers. We both quit smoking three years ago, and I'm surprised to see there are still cigarettes in the house. "I can't take it much longer," she warns me.

Finally, she finds what she's looking for, a book of matches. She tamps a cigarette out of the pack and lights up, inhaling jaggedly.

"What kind of a stunt is this?"

Her eyes train on me defiantly. "Maybe it's my turn to be stupid and self-destructive."

I proceed to list every stupid thing she's done in the last eleven years. I even make some up, stretch the truth a little to make my point. "But you don't see me complaining," I crow. "Sure, I'm difficult to live with sometimes. But at least one of us knows what it means to make a commitment. At least one of us was listening when the minister said for better, for worse."

"No question, you take the prize for stubbornness, Dan. Now if you could just learn when to quit." Robin is still glaring at me, but she doesn't look so cocky now. I note with satisfaction that her hand shakes when she draws the cigarette to her mouth.

"What did you think, everything was going to be easy?" I'm skidding wildly forward now, ranting like a drunk, spewing up rage. Out of the corner of my eye, I catch the dog slinking across the floor and cowering behind Robin's legs. "Things get a little rough and first thing, you're ready to pick up and leave town. Your husband doesn't turn out to be a star like you'd counted on, well, screw him. Or better yet, screw one of his friends." This last is below the belt, a coded reference to her one serious indiscretion, a night many years ago when she got drunk at a party and ended up in a locked bathroom with Gordon Hopper. She didn't commit adultery, but it is a technicality that rests uncomfortably on the question of how much further things might have gone had there been a second bathroom in the apartment.

"Well, I don't work that way," I bellow. "Like if someone's holding a knife on me, I think of you. I try to protect you. I don't hide under the bed and leave you out there to die. You're worse than an animal."

The words spray out of my mouth before I even know I've thought them. They shock me into silence. Across the room, Robin stares dazedly at the glowing tip of her cigarette. It is as though the eye of the storm has settled over us and sucked the air out of the room. The quiet feels oppressive and threatening.

"I was . . ." Her face contorts painfully as she tries to form the rest of the sentence. I think I hear the word "scared," but I may be imagining this. Then she twists away from me, hiding her face. Puck crawls out from under the desk and worms his way up into Robin's embrace. I reach out and touch her, but she flinches, so I hover there, the hun, the outsider, listening to her suck at the cigarette and exhale. Now that they are actually needed, I am stupidly at a loss for words; all I can think to say is "I'm sorry" and "I didn't mean it" over and over like some idiot Miss Manners. It's too late for apologies.

Robin carefully stubs the cigarette out in the dirt of her African violets and swivels around to face me.

"I'm going up to Camden." Her voice is flat. "Think what you want, Dan. But I was there for you." And then the coup de grâce. "Not that it matters. Because I'm through."

Here's what I'm hoping. We say these things and they're out, and whatever dark hole they flew out of, you can't stuff them back in. It doesn't even matter if they're not true, if you just said them in some kind of lunatic seizure. But I'm hoping that whatever it is between us, this cord that is anchored in our guts and that rips at my lungs when I've wounded her, I'm hoping that it's stronger than we are.

Another day, but from where I sit, in a molded plastic chair facing the door to the Rep's sanctum sanctorum, it looks weirdly like yesterday. On the way in, I passed Kyle McCann leaving. He had on the same pink shirt, the tie loosened to achieve exactly the same effect (rule number one for the call-back: wear whatever you wore before). He was also wearing the same self-satisfied look. The one my dad used to threaten to wipe off my face for me.

The big blond Cornhusker is here again, too, still nodding and gesturing and moving his lips. I briefly made a game of trying to identify the scenes he is reviewing, like charades, but he happened to catch me watching him and has retreated to a corner where I can't see his face.

I have broken rule number one by returning here in dry and pressed clothing, but I still probably look about as haggard as I did yesterday. I woke up about four this morning feeling seriously hungover, my muscles achy, and with a bleary sense of regret. Oh, yes, I remembered. What was it you said? That she was an animal? Nice work, you putz.

Robin was curled away from me, asleep. I considered waking her, getting this whole thing straightened out before she left for the day, but then thought better of it. Instead, I went out to the living room and watched CNN for an hour until I fell asleep on the couch. When I woke, the sun was glaring and she was gone.

After I get out of here, I'll give her a call. I'll offer to call Zak and weasel out of the first refusal. He won't be happy, and I can't imagine how I'm going to explain it. I forgot I had planned a vacation in Maine? The truth sounds too lame, so I'll have to come up with some plausible lie.

They call in the beefy blond; Eric Swanson is his name. He can't be reading for Terry, but he seems a little too fresh off the college football squad to play Hal. Who would take that guy seriously as a candidate for senator? On the other hand, maybe that's just what they're looking for, a Dan Quayle type.

This is just the kind of thinking that sabotages an audition before you even get in the door. Worrying about things that are out of your control. What if this, what if that? I've got plenty on my plate right now without dipping into the long view.

The door opens and Eric is ejected, looking like he just blew the game and would really like to pound something. I'm up.

When they bring me into the room, David Stover, the director, says "Ah, good to see you again, Dan," and the wax museum stirs perceptibly from out of a sluggish doze. They sit up in their chairs and turn their expectant smiles on me. "How about the scene with the reporter?" Stover suggests.

When you hit it out of the park the first time, everyone wants to see you do it again. So you go in and try to re-create that moment. You measure out the same pauses, repeat the same gestures. Every inflection is exactly as it was before—but lifeless. Dead. Deader than the wax museum's vacant gaze. You can't step into the same stream twice. Whoever said that, it's lamentably true.

The scene started out flat, I could feel it, but I'm chugging along, trying to pump some life into the corpse, gearing up for that moment in the scene where it sparked yesterday. But that moment comes and goes, and nothing. Stover takes a slug of his coffee and then stares into the bottom of the cup. Helen Wolfe, the casting director, lets her eyes wander to her watch. The only one still in the room with me is Arthur Haines, and he looks worried. Sweat begins to blur my vision, I've lost my place in the script. I can feel myself drowning up here, and the voice in my head is hysterical, screaming DON'T PANIC! DON'T PANIC! DON'T PANIC! DON'T PANIC! DON'T PANIC! DON'T PANIC! Then bingo, something clicks, and I let the water close over my head, I give in to the terror. Which happens to be exactly right for the scene. I'm underwater and I'm thrashing, but there's a rhythm to it now. I can feel the panic channeling into the character. The lines come from nowhere, spilling out of my mouth, one after another, as if I'd just thought of them. It doesn't get more real than that. I crash through to the end of the scene, my heart ricocheting off my ribs. A little over the top, but I've definitely got their attention.

We take a breather, sixty seconds or so to wipe the sweat out of my eyes and catch my breath. Shift gears, on to another section, this one at the beginning of the play. This time, things go more smoothly. I sail along, right past the first point where they might have cut me off. Good sign. Two pages, three, four, past another break, and all the way to Hal's exit.

At the end, Stover takes me back a few pages and gives me an adjustment.

"How about this section again, starting with Sheila's entrance. Pick up the cues faster this time. No pauses, no thinking. It should be rapid-fire, like screwball comedy."

This is not criticism; this is a sign of interest. It means "I'm thinking you're right for this, but before I sign you on, I need to know one thing: if I tell you to do something, can you just do it and not give me any crap about motivation?"

So we run it again, this time in high gear. I'm firing the lines at the reader, and she's batting them right back. Arthur Haines is nodding vigorously, and several times he barks with laughter. You gotta like a guy who's in your corner and doesn't make a secret of it.

Stover is more circumspect, but there are subtle tells if you know where to look.

He rubs his palms together briskly and makes a note.

Translation: You can take direction. Good. Great.

He asks Helen Wolfe a question, sotto voce, without taking his eyes off me.

Translation: Do we have to see anyone else for Hal? Or maybe, Who is his agent, again? Something along those lines.

Afterward, as I'm taking my leave, Helen turns her maternal smile on me.

"The play goes into rehearsal in two weeks. Would that present any conflicts for you?"

I feel that little ping a gambler gets when he's been dealt a flush. It's all I can do to keep from laughing giddily at the absurdity of the question. Of course, I don't have any conflicts, Helen. I haven't had a conflict in years. What I actually say, after a suitable pause, is that there's nothing that can't be changed.

And then a gesture that needs no translation: Haines winks.

It's three A.M. I'm watching Gene Kelly and Judy Garland in *For Me and My Gal*. They're a vaudeville team and just as they get their big break at the Palace, Kelly gets drafted. He slams his hand in a trunk so he can get a deferment, but his sacrifice isn't appreciated by Garland; in fact, she cuts him loose because he's put his career before his country. But it's a musical and it's Gene Kelly, so not to worry, they'll get back together in the end. The movie is pretty slight, but Kelly and Garland are so committed, they actually make the turkey fly by sheer force of will. When Judy Garland sings "How you gonna keep 'em down on the farm after they've seen Paree," she's practically pole-vaulting across the stage, her brow gleaming with sweat, her elbows pumping. In the Method-trained smugness of my youth, I was critical of performances this big, but nowadays I find I really like to see actors throwing themselves over the top. I want with all my heart to feel that simple exhilaration again. I'm tired of subtleties.

Robin is sleeping in the next room, and Puck has been patrolling the rooms all night. He'll come in here for a few minutes and start to settle down, and I can see him trying to forget about the suitcase parked next to the bedroom door. I tell him that it's okay, no one's abandoning him. "The two of us guys are going to batch it for a few days," I say with Gene Kelly–influenced joviality. He wags his tail limply, humoring me, then trundles back down the hall to check again on the status of the suitcase. Earlier, when I leashed him up, he hesitated at the door as though this might be some kind of trick. It was the shortest walk in years, one quick piss at the front door and then a dash back to the apartment to make sure she hadn't slipped off without us. His anxiety is palpable.

I know just how he feels. Theoretically, I got what I wanted—I'm staying here—but it's not sitting well on my stomach. This morning, I called Robin after the audition. I had worked out the beginnings of a nicely contrite little speech that would culminate in an offer to bag the whole commercial thing and just go up to her dad's place as planned.

"Last night was entirely my fault," I began and left a little opening for her to contradict me.

"It doesn't matter whose fault it was."

This wasn't the encouragement I had been hoping for, but I agreed that, no, it didn't matter. "What matters," I continued, "is that our marriage comes first. You're wrong to think that my career is more important." Actually, when I was imagining this conversation, I think I may have counted too heavily on her to jump in somewhere, but she seemed to be waiting for me to finish. "That's never been true."

"Okay." Her voice registered that, yes, she had heard me but she wasn't about to be taken in by a word of this malarkey. "I'm on another line. Can we talk about this tonight?"

"I'm working tonight, but, yeah, sure. Actually, I was just calling to say that if you want me to, I'll weasel my way out of the first refusal thing. We'll just go ahead and go."

She sighed audibly. "I don't want you to 'weasel' out of anything, Dan." And she hung up before I could backtrack and substitute the word "weasel" with something less, I don't know what, less weasely.

We never actually did talk about it. When I got home from work, she asked me how the audition went, showed polite interest when I told her that it went well, and then moved seamlessly into a laundry list of instructions on how to survive her absence—when to water and feed the various plants, which of the vets to speak to about Puck's medications, what was still at the dry cleaner's—instructions that might, it occurs to me now, be intended to keep the place running without her indefinitely. Her manner was pointedly casual and gracious.

I repeated my offer.

"I can call Zak in the morning and get out of this commercial thing. Honestly, I don't mind." And suddenly I didn't. Go figure.

Robin turned, and for a moment there I thought she might haul off and belt me, that or burst into tears. Whatever emotion she was struggling with, though, she managed to suffocate.

"No, it's probably best this way after all."

I don't know exactly what that means, except that it's the kind of line they used to give to Olivia de Havilland all the time. The wispy bravery of it was supposed to make you admire her gentle courage. But Robin is not the Olivia de Havilland type. She's more like Bette Davis, sarcastic and plucky and not about to let anyone step on her, thank you very much. This quiet restraint is unsettling.

So she's going up to Maine tomorrow where she'll spend the week with her family, kayaking, dining on lobster and mussels, generally lounging around the beach. I'm going to stay here, hunker down in front of the air conditioner and watch TV and maybe, if I'm lucky, spend a day dressed up in a rodent suit. Mulling it over, I'm having a hard time pin-pointing exactly what is in this for me. Of course, there's the money I stand to make if I book this commercial. But Robin is right: if I said that my choices were motivated by money, you'd take one look at my life and conclude that I was just about the stupidest person on the planet.

Garland and Kelly are doing a rousing finale, their arms locked, legs kicking, smiles beaming. It has nothing to do with being happy. It's not about making good choices. Eve-ryone knows that about Garland, but it's no less true of the rest of us. Actors act because we don't know what else to do.

While Robin was in the shower this morning, I took a peek in her suitcase and attempted to determine by its contents if she is leaving me for a week or for good. There was no con-clusive evidence either way, at least not on the top layer, and I knew better than to dig for clues, because I could never hope to reassemble the careful still life she had constructed: shirts stuffed with rolled socks, sweaters carefully folded, shoes wrapped in paper and tucked into the corners. One might wonder where in the wilds of Maine she anticipates wearing her red silk kimono. But, I consoled myself, if my ultimately practical wife had decided to leave me, surely my things would be packed, not hers.

Of course, I could have asked. But then she would have told me, and I just couldn't bring myself to tempt fate like that. So, instead, I pretended that everything was fine. I walked her downstairs to the waiting car service and put her bag in the trunk. I told her to have a good time. She gave me the pressed lip, indulgent smile I've seen her give store clerks or waiters when she decides it's not worth making a fuss. "You, too."

I got back up to the apartment and checked the answering machine, in case Zak had called while I was downstairs. Nothing. Then I went back to bed. I haven't done this in years, slept during the day. It is one of the many little disciplines, the seemingly inconsequential rules I made up for my life as an actor. They are the things that distinguish me from a bum. I don't sleep during the day. I don't drink or watch TV before five. I get up at a reasonable hour, do half an hour with the weights or go for a run, shave and dress, and then leave the house. I do something productive, preferably career-related, but if not, then anything concrete and improving, even if it's as small as picking up the groceries. I tell myself that all this matters, that even more than the rent money I bring in bartending, these habits are what keep me from being a nothing.

But I was so tired. It was as though the sleep I have been losing for the last several weeks caught up with me all at once. I was suddenly and completely exhausted. I made some pretense of reading the paper, sitting upright at the table and jerking awake every few minutes when my chin dropped. What the hell, I finally told myself, you're supposed to be on vacation. You can do whatever you please. Who's to stop you? No one. Puck followed me into the bedroom, and I hoisted him up with me. It's been some time since he's been able to leap up on the furniture. When I lifted him, I was careful to cradle his haunches. He remained gingerly stiff in my arms. It may not have been worth the bother for him, but I wanted his company.

Sometime later, I am swimming to consciousness in a groggy panic, dragging the empty lake of the mattress for a body. Gone. I don't know what I am missing, but it is critical. I try to recall the last fragments of a dream, but they are drifting back beneath the surface. The room is still and stuffy, the late afternoon light oppressively bright behind the blinds. From the park, I pick out the sounds of children. They are chanting something—duck, duck, goose?—and, inexplicably, I am weepy and nostalgic for my life. I have the conviction, I couldn't tell you why, that my life is shifting underneath me, changing radically, right this minute. I can't even say for better or worse. It could be that Robin is working herself up to leave me, or already has, and I'm just too thick to know it. Or perhaps my career is about to really take off and I'm going to reap the rewards of years of patience and hard work. And this, oddly, is almost as terrifying.

Everyone has these moments, I suppose, when you feel you're on the cusp of something big, that any minute now the wave you're riding will crest and you'll be able to see into your future. In my limited experience, the expectation is misguided—you reach that peak and what you see is a trough and beyond that another big wave obscuring your vision. The message here is probably more mundane, something along the lines of "Avoid afternoon naps."

I check the answering machine. Just in case I didn't hear the phone ringing. Nothing. Nothing from Robin, who promised to call when she got in, nothing from the agent. Nothing. Today is Wednesday. I auditioned yesterday. There's no reason why I should hear from Tribeca before Friday. Even next week. They may still be seeing people. Certainly not before Friday. It's ridiculous to worry until then.

The commercial is a different kettle of fish. I definitely should have heard something by now, if they need to do a fitting, sign contracts, whatever. It's what, four-thirty, so Zak probably won't call today. I can't completely rule it out yet, maybe in the morning. If I don't hear tomorrow, then I'll have to assume they went with someone else and this whole fracas with Robin was completely pointless. They could at least call, put me out of my misery. I mean, they have to know by now. Unless the person they want to use is dicking them around. Who knows? This whole thing is so last-minute, cast and shoot the same week. But definitely, if I don't hear by tomorrow afternoon, then I don't have it.

I stare at the phone for a bleary stretch of time, as though it may ring if I just sit here long enough. So what, if Robin said she'd call? Who am I, some prickly teenager that I should care who calls whom? And the answer here would have to be yes, because I don't pick up the phone right away.

Instead, in a precise imitation of adolescent angst, I rehearse variations on an imaginary phone conversation. I try on the indignant role and discard it because, even in my own ears, I sound petulant. I try casual, just ringing up to see how you're getting on, hot enough for you, blah, blah, blah.

I pick up the phone and dial out the number Robin has left in case of emergency. It rings four times, and then a robotic female voice announces the number and suggests I leave a message. "Robin, it's Dan." I wait, hoping that maybe someone will pick up. "Okay, when you get a chance, give me a call. No big deal, I just want to know you got in okay."

It's five o'clock, and the evening looms empty in front of me. The movie channel is showing *On the Town* at eight, and I'm not knocking it, it's a good movie, even with Ann Miller, but there's only so many times you can watch even the good ones, and I've seen it a few more times than that.

What I need to do, I tell myself, is to get off my duff. Get out of the house, call up some friends, do a guys' night out. Having a plan invigorates me. I dial up my buddy Keith and get his machine. "You've reached the home of Sarah and Keith. There's a beep coming up and then you're on." "Keith, it's Dan. Are you there? Okay, well, it's about five, and I'm thinking it's a good night to do a little carousing. Call me for further details." Then I call Mike Hardin, whom I haven't seen in a long time but have been meaning to call, who, his message informs me, is in Vermont doing summer stock until Labor Day. Then Stuart Hoffman, who is away from his desk, and Barry Ingles, who can be a real jerk sometimes but whose name is entered right beneath Stuart's in my address book. Barry's answering machine has one of those endless musical selections preceding the beep. I wait out the first minute but then hang up. I'm half tempted to call the operator, just to confirm that it's not faulty equipment, that in fact every person on the planet but me is occupied.

When the phone rings, the sound startles me. Before I pick up the receiver, I take a deep breath to collect myself and I repeat in my head a brief incantation-slash-affirmation: you deserve good things.

"Dan-O." Stuart's rumbly bass booms over the line. "Got your message. You okay?"

"Sure."

"What's going on?"

"Oh, nothing much." The master of understatement. "I was just thinking about coming into the city, and I wondered if you were up for a little libation and conversation."

"What, now?" He pauses, then asks again. "What's up?" His voice is quietly insistent, as though I have bad news to spring on him, and I may as well cut to the chase. I suspect this is a habit he developed from years of talking with doctors.

"Nothing's up. Robin's up in Maine for a few days, and I'm just not in the mood to sit home."

"She went up there alone?"

"No, not alone." I'm trying to remember if I said anything in my message that would put Stuart on high alert like this. "She's with her dad and his wife. I was going to go, but I'm on first refusal for a commercial, so I have to sit tight until Friday."

"So you're all alone in the city, huh, big boy?" Apparently satisfied, Stuart reverts to the banter we established years and years ago, when he played Falstaff to my Prince Hal at the Dallas Shakespeare festival. The play more or less set a tone for our friendship in that he still likes to pretend that his job in life is to corrupt me. That he is gay supposedly makes him privy to all kinds of depravity; the fact that I am straight and, better yet, from Oklahoma makes me forever the innocent rube.

In fact, he's always led a very conventional and quiet life. Even when he was still acting, he was the designated adult in our group, the only one with a steady partner, dental insurance, matching glassware, all the markers of responsible living. When Andre got sick, Stuart stopped taking out-of-town jobs and gradually got hooked into this company that does books on tape. He started off just reading the books, but gradually slid over to the production side, too, because they needed the insurance coverage. Now he goes to work every morning and is probably home and in bed by nine most nights.

I take the subway in, and when we pull into Wall Street, the car fills with a swarm of worker bees heading home. It's probably still in the low eighties on the street and a good ten degrees warmer in here. A hundred upraised arms perfume the tired air. At each stop, the doors open and more bodies squeeze in. One Wall Street hustler uses his briefcase as a battering ram, letting the doors bump open and shut until he can press himself into the last inch of open space on the inside of the car. I am wedged against a young woman with plump bare arms. Behind her, a man with his suit coat flung tiredly over his shoulder holds up a wilted copy of the *Post* with his free hand. We are all immodestly close, and each time the train lurches around a curve, slows or speeds up, we are flung against the warm flesh of our neighbors. The woman and I are both pretending mightily, she that her breasts are not pressed into my stomach, I that the Yankees' win over the Angels is gripping reading.

Stuart and I have made plans to meet at McLeary's, one of the old hangouts on Amsterdam. It's a typical Irish bar, sawdust on the floor, greasy sausages in a warming tray for happy hour, cheap and friendly and one of the few reminders that the neighborhood was working class not too long ago. The owner has hung some ferns in the window and put out a few tables on the sidewalk to siphon off the yuppies who now stream up and down the avenue at night, but the clientele seems unchanged from twenty, thirty years ago. A half-dozen grizzled old men watch the Yankees game at the bar; a couple younger ones flirt with an orange-haired woman in a thigh gripping miniskirt. They are like Eugene O'Neill characters in *The Iceman Cometh*, preserved in the smoky amber tar that coats every surface of the bar. I don't recognize anyone except Stuart, sitting at a table near the jukebox. He grins and leaps to his feet, arms open to embrace me.

"Hey, you're looking good, Stu," I tell him, slapping his back with one hand and patting his gut with the other, a guy hug. He's built like an opera tenor, big and barrel-chested. He played Falstaff without padding and even did Santa for Macy's one year. ("Don't let me do that again, not if you care for me," he said afterward with jokey terror.) Then when Andre was withering away, Stuart responded by bulking up even more, eating both portions of whatever dish he'd whipped up to tempt Andre.

"I'm going to the gym three times a week. I hate it," he moans, but he seems pleased that I've noticed. "I pedal and pedal and pedal. It's so boring. They have videotapes where you can bike the back roads of France, but you can't pull over and eat a nice little lunch of pâté and cheese and champagne. So where's the fun in that?"

I get us a pitcher from the bar, and we settle back into the drowsy glow of a late August evening. We talk and we watch the passing scene outside: the couples locked in heated conversations, the men in dark glasses and the gorgeous women who are palpably aware of being watched, the skinny guy hawking designer watches and keeping one eye peeled for the cops. The drone of the sportscasters is soothing, a white noise surging now and then with the derisive hoots of the patrons at the bar, and I'm tipsy well before we've drained the first pitcher. I'm having a good time. We're yakking about the shows we've seen lately, who's good in what, who stinks, who we would have cast instead.

"Speaking of which," Stuart is saying, "I saw Marylou on a rerun of *Chicago Hope* last week. Did you see it? She was doing the sister of this guy who's dying of some disease."

Marylou Kolodejchuk, a.k.a. Marilou Cole, a.k.a. the woman with whom I spent a few besotted, pre-Robin years until she made a pilgrimage out to LA for pilot season and just never bothered to come back.

"She fell back on that old plucky-through-the-tears thing she does, but she was pretty good. God, remember that night she waltzed through the back wall of the set?"

We stroll down memory lane, Stuart and I, with Marylou waltzing and Jim Callahan listening to the Yankees games backstage and Sarkowski with that ratty old pea coat he wore everywhere, even to the Tonys that year, and Amanda and that boyfriend of hers, what was his name, the one who turned out to be freshly sprung from Bellevue, arguing at the top of their lungs on the street in front of Steve's until someone in an upstairs apartment began pelting them with garbage. And then there was the time Amanda and Robin made fried chicken and mashed potatoes at three in the morning, and all of us sat around drinking Jack Daniel's and eating chicken and telling stories. And the time we drove down to Louisville in Gordy Hopper's Electra 88 with the busted muffler and the ice cubes for air-conditioning. And the time

Karl went up in the middle of his monologue and asked someone in the front row if she had seen the play before and did she happen to remember his next line.

Most of these people aren't around anymore. Karl's out in LA now, too, manages a plant care business, waters houseplants for all the Hollywood muckety-mucks. Calls Stuart periodically, tells him whose plants he's doing, that Kathleen Turner keeps killing her ferns, doesn't know what she does to them, but they're brown as cockroaches in two weeks. Amanda married a tree farmer and moved to New Hampshire, has four-year-old twins. Jim and Dorrie Callahan moved out to Denver, so there's a standing invitation to come and ski anytime. Steve died. Hopper went back to Baltimore after his dad's stroke, took over the family's office supplies business. Then Andre, Stuart's lover, died. The knot of our circle keeps shrinking. It used to be we could make a few calls and get up a crowd on a few hours' notice, a night hanging out here at McLeary's, shooting pool, or a spontaneous party at one of a half-dozen apartments on the Upper West Side. Or Sarkowski's place on West Forty-fifth, which was decorated like a frat house, someone always passed out on the couch or hanging out between auditions, amazing to think that his beach house was actually in *Architectural Digest* last year. Nowadays, any kind of gathering requires weeks of planning and then the evening ends somewhere before ten because there are babysitters and morning appointments and long drives back to Jersey.

"What the hell happened?" I blurt this out with such passion that I look around to see if anyone else has taken note. It has gotten dark while we were talking and the game has ended. I suspect I am drunk.

"Things change, Danny boy."

"The thing is . . ." I pause here because I can't quite place what the thing is. "The thing is, I'm starting to think like this is it, one way or the other. This is my last shot. If I get this part at Tribeca, then that's a pretty clear sign, don't you think?"

Stuart is listening, nodding slowly, but he's not convinced.

"If I don't get it"—the possibility fills me with such anticipatory grief that I have to wait for my throat to open again before I can speak—"if I don't get it, well, I guess that's a pretty clear sign, too."

"What's it say?" Stuart asks.

"Hmm?"

"The sign. What's it say?"

"You're a failure, pal. Pick up your marbles and go home. Move to Santa Fe and get a job and make your wife a happy woman."

There's nothing to say to this. He can't tell me to buck up, that if not this job, then something else will come along. We know better, old soldiers that we are. And he certainly can't tell me that it's time to call it a day, even if it is. We sit with the silence, mulling it all over.

There's an old joke, goes like this: two actors sitting in a bar—maybe not a bar, but for symmetry's sake, let's say a bar—and they're lamenting the sad state of the theater. One says to the other, "You know, I haven't worked in almost two years." The other one says, "Yeah, I haven't had a job in three years." And the first one takes another swig of his beer and says, "Man, I wish we could get out of this fucking business."

So, it's three in the morning, and I'm lying in bed, trying to recall if my hamster, Buffy, scratched his ear with his back paw or his front paw. I'm thinking it was his back paw, like a dog, in which case I'm going to have to sacrifice reality because I can't get my own leg anywhere near my head.

Zak called this morning. Tomorrow, I report bright and early to the old Astoria Studios in Queens for the Dobbins Copier commercial. "What'd I tell you, Zak," I blurted out. "The old dog still has a few tricks left in him." Turns out, these tricks do not include scratching my ear with my foot. Not that it actually matters.

They messengered the copy to me this afternoon. I hadn't seen the storyboards for this thing, so I really wasn't clear on what the commercial was about, except that it somehow figured a rodent and a copy machine. It turns out to be a cross-cut kind of thing, back and forth between me, affectionately referred to as Lab Rat, whose copier jams and shreds paper, and another guy, Office Worker, the one dressed in a stylish-looking business suit, the one who bought a Dobbins. In the first shot, Lab Rat is sniffing curiously around a copier, lifting levers, pulling open doors. This is where I'm thinking an ear scratch would be a nice piece of business. Then cut to Office Worker casually loading a stack of documents into the feeder. Then Lab Rat, and he's running on one of those hamster wheels. Then a couple of shots of the copier and all its features. Then back to Lab Rat on the wheel again. Next shot is Office Worker chatting on the phone, feet up on his desk. Finally, Lab Rat lying belly up on the wheel, hysterical and exhausted. And then some artwork with the Dobbins logo.

All the dialogue is in voice-over, so I don't have any lines to worry about. Nothing to worry about, I keep telling myself. A couple of squeaks, a couple of turns on the ol' hamster wheel, and I'm out of there. Piece of cake.

Puck is pawing at the side of the mattress, letting me know that he needs to go out. I roll away from him but then feel guilty, imagining his sorrowful eyes watching my back and waiting. He's developed the patience of Buddha, this dog. When he was younger, he'd get half his exercise before we even got out the door. An elaborate dance of solicitation, prancing toward the door and then circling back until I put on my shoes and followed him. When the leash came out of the closet, his eagerness would crest into a volley of frenzied yelps and leaps, and he'd spin in skidding circles on the parquet. Now he waits quietly, trusting me to do the right thing.

Robin and I are playing phone tag. When I got in last night, there were two hang-ups on the machine, a message from Hal—sorry he missed me, out for a run, but, yeah, let's get together some time—another hang-up, then a message from Robin.

"Dan?" There was a pause, while she waited for me to pick up. When I didn't, she announced the time, one-thirty in the morning, in what I'm guessing is the exact same tone of exasperation that her mother used with her however many years ago. And then another pause before her tone shifted to brisk. "Okay. I'm just returning your call. I'll be around in the morning if you want to talk, but then we're heading out. Okay, then."

I tried to calculate how early was too early to call, but I misjudged on one side or the other because at eight this morning, I got their answering machine again. "Hi, it's Dan again," I began, and suddenly I was imagining a scene on the receiving end of my phone call. With the clarity of a psychic, I could see Robin and Jack and Mina, all of them pink with sunburn and still in their pajamas, and they're eating their granola and sipping their coffee while my voice rattles over the machine. "Sorry about last night. I was out with Stuart. Haven't heard on the commercial yet. But I was thinking, hey, maybe I could rent a car and drive up there Saturday. Let me know what you think. Hey Jack, Mina. Catching any fish, Jack? So give me a call when you get a chance, sweetie. We're doing great down here. Puck misses you." Even before I hung up, I was wishing there was some way to erase the tape and start over. This time, try to sound a little less like a used car salesman. And lose the pathetic line about

Puck. What was that supposed to mean? The dog misses you, but I'm doing fine?

The dog.

I lurch upright and search the floor for my shoes. Puck's tail thumps twice in gratitude. He follows me down the hall and, when I hook the leash onto his collar, makes a sort of stiff-legged curtsy, a substitute for sitting and then having to clamber all the way up again. I find the keys on the hall table, stuff a couple of plastic bags into the pocket of my shorts, and we head out to the elevator.

Our building is old and slightly shabby, but if one can look past the naked bulb on the landing and the gouged and whitewashed walls, there are still hints of its grander beginnings. The worn marble landing is the size of a spacious studio apartment, and the scrolled plaster ceilings are twelve feet, echoing a time when space was not at such a premium. The building is rent-controlled, so nothing has changed in years, not the tenants, not the paint.

While we're waiting for the elevator, I hear what sounds like movement behind Mrs. Doherty's door. There's no light coming from under the doorsill, but I wouldn't be surprised if, even at this hour, she is eyeballing me through her peephole, alerted by the groans and squeaks of the elevator as it heaves its way up from the ground floor. She leaves her apartment only every few days for groceries, pushing her wire cart in front of her like a walker and glaring at me suspiciously whenever I greet her. When we first moved in,

I tried to win her over with friendliness, but six years later, she persists in regarding me warily, as though I might one day force her back into her dusty foyer and rob her of all the china figurines and crocheted doilies that can be seen crowding the dim interior of her rooms. Robin has gradually gained her confidence, however, at least enough to discover that her first name is Mary, that she raised three children here, and that she can recite the dates and apartment numbers of every burglary, every change of tenants through death or divorce, every mishap that has occurred in this building over the last several decades. Until our break-in, the fourth floor held the record for the fewest burglaries. "And none of them came in through an open window." Robin thought she heard accusation in Mary's voice, as though our carelessness has spoiled it for everybody.

The elevator is one of the slowest rides in the city, and while we descend, Puck paces the confines of the bronze cage, in a hurry to get outside and relieve his aging bladder. I am nowhere near so eager. This late-night descent into the streets charges me with enough adrenaline to keep me alert for the rest of the night. As we emerge from the relative safety of the building, I check both ways down the avenue. That I don't see anyone in no way eases my anxiety. Puck, oblivious, lifts his leg and drowns a weed that has sprung up through a crack in the concrete.

It is actually a beautiful street, edged on this side by graceful limestone buildings and, on the far side, by Prospect

Park. All of the buildings but ours have gone co-op over the past ten years, sandblasting the grime from their gargoyles and unfurling fresh awnings onto the avenue. But the quiet prosperity is misleading. This pocket of gentrification is a scant few subway stops from half the projects in Brooklyn and an inviting destination spot for the criminally minded. The length of the avenue is a particular favorite with muggers, because they can hit their target and then disappear into the foresty expanse of the park across the street. Last winter, a man on the second floor was held up at gunpoint right where I'm standing, in the shadow of our awning.

We move into the peachy glow of the sodium streetlights, and Puck shuffles slowly toward the curb. The curb glitters with safety glass, where car windows have been smashed in search of phones and tape decks. I wait impatiently while he sniffs the leg of a newspaper box and then waters it. Next is the bus stop sign, and then the light pole and mailbox on the corner. Usually, this is as far as we go at night, just twenty paces to the corner and back, but it takes a good ten minutes to inspect and mark each stop on the route. When I try to hurry him, he gives me a wounded look and, I swear it, exaggerates the arthritic stiffness in his gait. Then he gives his end of the leash a small tug toward the tree trunks down the slope.

Something is fluttering from a lower limb of the old plane tree. I can't make it out from this distance, but then I notice that the trees all the way down the block are festooned with paper. On closer inspection, they turn out to be crayoned drawings of the trees themselves: row after row of green lollipops, some with bluebirds and yellow ball suns. "Save Our Trees" is lettered in a careful, childish hand across this first one. Taped to the next trunk is another drawing, but its message is lost in the deep shadows.

Early this spring, a utility crew showed up unannounced and started surveying the block to install new pipeline. The project would entail digging into the gnarled root system that underlies the entire length and width of the block. From the city's perspective, the old trees are a nuisance anyway—their roots curdle the sidewalks and push up asphalt—but when they blithely started ribboning off old willow oaks and plane trees, they severely underestimated the depth of the neighborhood's affection for those trees. They also didn't take into consideration that half the newly renovated brownstones are inhabited by attorneys with inflated property values to protect. Wham bam, the city was up to its eyeballs in court injunctions before they could even finish staking.

A sheet of butcher paper has been wrapped around one trunk about eye level and secured with tape. I have to walk around the trunk to read the length of the message: "This tree was planted in 1927. It will take another . . ."

There is movement in the shadows. I feel the presence of another human being before I see him. A dark silhouette. He is maybe fifteen paces off, coming down the sidewalk in my direction, but even at this distance I can tell he is not one of the attorneys coming home late. When he sees that I have spotted him, his gait becomes exaggeratedly casual.

He is thin, I see now, and his clothes are several sizes too large. They hang off him like a scarecrow. Enormous jeans ride low on his hips and drag at the heels of absurdly large and elaborate running shoes. It is the uniform of clowns and young urban wannabes.

I see him glance around, checking for other eyes that might be watching us. My limbs fill with helium. I tighten my grip on Puck's leash and try to redirect us slowly toward the curb, toward the light, casual, as though I'm not avoiding him, oh no, I just happen to live on the other side of the street. I'm not going to make it, not without running. I stiffen my spine as we prepare to pass one another, and my eyes move to his.

It's him. The guy in my apartment. A small flinch betrays that he recognizes me, too. You fuck. You fucking son of a bitch. Hold a knife on me in my own fucking kitchen. Not again, you shithead. No way, you fucking piece of shit. The words are coming out of my mouth. His cocky swagger wilts, and he edges around me, mumbling something. Once past, he breaks into a light trot.

I drop Puck's leash and yell at him to sit and stay and, I don't know, maybe I'm yelling at the guy to stay, I'm so crazy with rage, I don't know. I follow him. I break into a run and charge after him down the block. I don't know what I'm thinking, my heart is thundering and pumping gallons of blood into my head so I can't think. I just run.

He sprints across Eighth Avenue and I follow, checking for cars, but there is only one and it is too far down the avenue to help or hurt. He cuts left, and we are pounding along Eighth. We cross Fifth Street, then Sixth, then Seventh, and I figure he must be heading for the subway station two blocks ahead. I don't think I'm going to make it that far. There is a painful stitch gathering in my side, and my breath is coming in searing gasps. I have my eyes trained on his back and I can hear him panting, too, but he is also starting to put distance between us. And then he stumbles. His gawky limbs buckle and he flies sprawling onto the pavement. I am on top of him before he has a chance to get up. He flails, and one elbow connects, hard, with my cheekbone. I scrabble back onto my feet and kick him once, feebly, but then when he starts to rise, I kick him again, harder, and again, I don't know how often, until he crumples, shielding his face. I find my breath enough to croak a few more obscenities at him.

"I wasn't doing nothing," he whimpers. "I didn't do nothing to you."

Something is wrong. Something is drastically wrong here. The voice. I have been hearing a voice in my head for the past month—"I got a gun"—the timbre of that voice, every inflection, the curl of each vowel and the thud of every consonant is burnished into my nightmares. This is not the same voice.

I look down at this guy I've been chasing. He is rising slowly, warily, to his knees, one hand cradling his jaw, and though he is the same race and has the same lanky build as my burglar, he is not the same man. For starters, this is a kid, fifteen, sixteen at most. And he's trying not to cry. His mouth is smeared with blood.

He senses the moment has shifted and suddenly springs up and back, turns heel and takes off again, a jagged painful lope punctuated every few feet by a glance backward to see if I am in pursuit.

I feel sick in my gut. I've attacked someone with no provocation, no excuse in the world, and beat him on the street. I am deeply ashamed. I am dust. There are no words for this.

I am squatted on the steps of a brownstone, hunched over and waiting for the earth to swallow me up when a voice hails me from above.

"Are you okay?" An old man, clad in bathrobe and slippers, is standing on the stoop of the brownstone, just inside his doorway. He is framed in the yellow light of the vestibule.

I nod mutely. My throat is closed.

"Do you want me to call the police?" He moves down a few steps, letting the door shut behind him. "I saw him take off. He can't be too far. I can call the police for you. No trouble."

It takes me a second before I understand. He believes he has witnessed a mugging. That I am the victim.

"No. No police."

He shrugs, puzzled, and takes another look at me. "You live around here?"

"Third and the Park."

"Ah, that's nice, those buildings up there."

"Yeah." Into my aching head swims a picture of my block and the recollection that I've left Puck sitting on the sidewalk there. Who knows how long he will stay before he tires of it and realizes he can just walk away. We've never tested his obedience this far.

"You're going to have some shiner to show for your troubles tomorrow."

My fingers find the tender swelling along my cheekbone where I caught the kid's elbow. "I'm fine."

"Well, if you're sure you're gonna be okay."

I pull myself to my feet. "Thanks."

It is a long walk home. A breeze has come up and is sending bits of trash and newspaper skirting up the street. I move blindly, passing in and out of shadow. I know that people have done worse. In the scheme of things, this is minor league barbarity. But I know what it feels like now. I've tasted what I'm capable of. Somewhere past Fifth Street, a plastic grocery bag is rattling in the branches of a tree. I keep walking until I turn up my familiar street and spy Puck in the distance, still sitting, waiting for me to come back. He wags his tail in welcome, and my grief bursts open like a melon.

*　　　　　*　　　　　*

It is luck I don't deserve that I'm wearing a mask for this commercial. By dawn, my right eye has swollen to a slit. Through my good eye—good being a relative term here to describe an eye that is red and rheumy with sleeplessness but otherwise normal—I survey the damage in the bathroom mirror. There isn't much to be done about the swelling, but I reason that a little makeup might at least tone down some of the more garish shades of purple blooming on the right side of my face. I'm operating on maybe two hours' sleep and so buzzy that my hand shakes when I dab pancake under the eye.

Among my repertoire of nontransferable job skills, I know how to create a completely convincing bruise with makeup. All kinds of disfigurations, in fact, along with the standard old-age lines and pouches. Covering up a bruise is much harder, though, and I make a mess of it. In addition to the swelling, I now appear to have some rare skin disease, perhaps the early stages of leprosy. On the train out to Queens, I think I catch people eyeing me circumspectly, giving me a wide berth.

Within five minutes of my showing up for my call at Astoria Studios, the production assistant has come striding down the hall, a stiffly perky blonde who sizes me up in a glance. One look confirms everything she already knows about actors, that we're unreliable children who have to be coddled because of union rules.

"You must be Dan." She scribbles something on a clip-board and then presents me with a Junior League smile and her name, which sounds like Teacup but is more likely Teeka or Teega. "That looks nasty. Does it hurt?"

"I'm fine," I tell her. "A little run-in with a mugger last night."

"How awful. Are you okay to work?" The question might seem casual, but her bullshit antennae are up and waving.

"Absolutely." I resist the impulse to elaborate, to weave some long and babbling defense of my competence. But this is all she wanted to know, that I'm not going to flake out and make her morning a living hell. Now that we've cleared that up, her features relax into a semblance of sympathy.

"You poor thing. Where did this happen?"

"Outside my home. Park Slope."

She shakes her head and confides, "My friend got mugged on Madison and Eighty-first last year in broad daylight. It just goes to show." What it might go to show, she leaves for me to figure out. "Well, all I can say is thank goodness you're wearing that costume, right? So, okay." She consults her clipboard. "I left the contracts in your dressing room. Jodi—" She waves over a waifish girl in skintight pants and an ab-breviated T-shirt that look as though they were purchased for someone even smaller and thinner. When she lisps hello, she ducks her head and peers up at me with raccoon-lined eyes. "Jodi can show you where your dressing room is. They won't need you on the set for an hour or so. There're break-fast goodies on the catering table. Are you hungry? Excuse me." The two-way radio on her hip is bleating, and after a brief exchange that includes a reference to the talent—that would be me—she glances surreptitiously at me and then steps out of earshot before continuing the conversation.

My stomach rumbles at the mere mention of food and reminds me that I haven't eaten since . . . when? Yester-day, sometime yesterday. I'm buzzing with exhaustion and hunger and nerves. That's what this is, the jitters. After all these years, the preface to performance is still a heightened anxiety, like a motor running too fast. It doesn't matter what the role is, whether it's Broadway or, in this case, a no-liner rodent on a commercial. You'd think I could learn to relax. Then again, I did a show once with an actress whose name you would recognize, who'd been in the business at least thirty years and still, every night at five minutes to curtain, would disappear into the bathroom and empty the contents of her stomach.

Teeka returns, saying, "Change of plans. They want you on the set."

I'm escorted to a cavernous soundstage, past the catering table where half a dozen stagehands are scarfing down muf-fins and shooting the breeze, and through the clutch of suits who represent the agency and the client. The appearance of a one-eyed actor causes a stir. I can hear the whispered hor-ror in my wake, but Teeka drops back to soothe and reassure them. "Thank goodness he's wearing that costume," she repeats. Yes, yes, we're all in agreement on that stroke of good fortune.

The set is something Kafka might dream up. Three walls of a room-sized cage have been constructed. Against the back wall is an enormous copier. Next to it, they've strapped a watercooler onto the bars of the cage. Strapped to another wall is a red-framed mirror and a large plastic chute filled with giant brown pellets, and from the ceiling hangs a big blue bell. The floor of the set is knee-deep in shredded paper. But the centerpiece of the set is a metal contraption, something like a small Ferris wheel. A half-dozen people are gathered watching a stagehand slowly revolve the wheel with his hands; he grabs a spoke and gives it a good pull, like Vanna White on *Wheel of Fortune*. Then a voice from up in the lights yells at him to hold. He stops the wheel with some effort, and they wait, staring up into the dark.

"Nope, we're still getting too much light off it," the voice in the rafters yells. The group pauses and mulls this over. There's a palpable tension on the set. Everyone is glancing surreptitiously at a man in knife-pleated khakis and a lemon yellow polo shirt. When he turns around, I recognize the director. He is small and wiry and would probably identify himself as a serious runner. I'm guessing he's about my age, but his hairline has already receded, leaving behind an island of wispy, colorless hair that floats above his creased forehead. At the moment, his face is taut with concentration or suppressed anger, his already thin lips pressed into a straight line. He squints at us, then holds up a finger to indicate he will be with us in a moment.

"Okay, so you have to matte the surface? How long will that take?" He is staring at his watch, and because he isn't looking at anyone, there is a pause while the group decides who should answer. After a brief conference, they decide the paint job will take forty minutes, so they can do a run-through with me first.

The director then turns back to us and makes a fairly obvious shift to a friendly public persona. "Dan, good to see you again. Chris Pitney." He thrusts out a hand and shakes, vigorously and a fraction of a minute too long. "Boy, they got you good. Can you see out of that eye?"

"Yeah. No problem."

"Next time, just give them your wallet. I had a neighbor tried to negotiate with some thug for his ID. Ended up with a knife in his side." I nod to indicate I'm filing this away— give them your wallet.

"No costume?" Again, the question seems not to be di- rected at anyone in particular, so I'm not sure if I should answer. Teeka jumps in that she can have Wardrobe bring it down to the set.

"No. Never mind. Well, just the paws. The rest we can do without for now. It's probably cooler under the lights without it."

He refocuses on me. "So Dan, let's get you on the wheel. Just hop up there and get the feel of moving on it."

A stagehand holds the wheel still while I climb through the spokes and onto the wheel. There is a floor, if you will, of foam-covered bars spaced about a foot apart. I crouch on all fours and slowly advance to the next bar, one hand at a time, following with my feet. After a few false starts where I lose my footing and bang a shin, I start to get the hang of it. It's like climbing a ladder, except that the ladder is moving underneath me, pushing me forward. I fall into an easy rhythm, alternate feet and hands working in sync. Pitney encourages me to pick up the speed.

"What you're doing is great, Dan. But we need a sense of urgency, a frantic quality. Maybe if you put more into the shoulders."

Because I have no peripheral vision on my right side, I can't see Pitney, but I can hear in his tone that he would just love to jump up here and show me how to make this baby spin. I start treading a little faster, and almost immediately, sweat beads on my forehead and begins to trickle down my ribs. I don't have a clue what he has in mind with my shoulders, so instead I try nosing my head side to side in quick little staccato motions. This is good, I can tell, and I hear what sounds like an approving murmur from the small crowd that has gathered at the edge of the set. A drop of sweat slides into my left eye and blurs what's left of my vision and I stop, gripping the bars as the wheel swings first up and then back, before coming to rest.

"That's good. Great. Don't go past your limit. We can always speed up the film if we have to."

A dark, parrot-nosed woman dressed in pink overalls has emerged through the knot of observers and approaches Pitney with what looks to be an armful of stuffed animals.

"Oh, good. I'm sorry, what's your name? Sheila? Sheila here has your paws. Go ahead and put those on and we'll run this one more time. Frank, how's it looking?"

The paws are made of smooth white fake fur and have long prehensile toes ending in claws. On the undersides of one pair are pink cotton gloves. The other pair are designed to strap over my shoes. Sheila helps me Velcro the paws into place, and I hold up my hands in front of me, slowly examining them with exaggerated horror.

"Can this be evil?" I intone and then laugh maniacally. There are a few obliging chuckles around the set. No telling how many of them recognize an imitation of Spencer Tracy's Jekyll and Hyde and how many think I'm just another loosely hinged actor. I catch Jodi, Teeka's assistant, watching me intently and sucking on a strand of hair. I wink at her, and her eyes drift to the floor.

"Okay, whenever you're ready . . ." Pitney is smiling, but it's a thin smile of tolerance. He doesn't have time for fooling around. I get the sense that this is a break for him, too, the chance to do a big-budget national instead of the local RV and furniture warehouse ads. He may even have private fantasies that this will break him out, that it will lead to bigger things, a TV pilot or who knows what else. Of course, he's wrong. This is a job, nothing else, a couple days' work, and at best it will lead to more days just like this one. I could tell him, relax, your life isn't in here. It's outside that door, out in the world somewhere. This? This is ridiculous. But would he listen to the one-eyed actor with the rat paws? Not a chance.

I climb back up on the wheel, my rat nails clattering against metal, and begin climbing the wheel. The paws take a little getting used to, but they also help me visualize myself as Lab Rat. I pick up speed and start the sniffing motions and manage to keep all these balls in the air until Pitney says "Cut." Again, the wheel slows to a halt and I can see a half-circle of satisfied mugs, some encouraging nods. We're in business.

Next, we run the final shot. Pitney instructs me to lie on my back on the wheel. "What we're looking for here is an exhausted rat. But also at the end of his rope. Really crazed."

"In other words, just be yourself, Dan," I joke, but of course, no one knows if I'm kidding or not, so they smile uncertainly, humoring me.

I lie back, raising my legs and arms above me, and start slowly bicycling my feet and twitching a bit, squeaking pathetically.

I'm practically giddy with sleeplessness and disdain, and who knows, this may be working in my favor. Whatever impulse comes to me, I follow it. I feel like Steve Martin or

Robin Williams, ricocheting in high gear from one new piece of business to the next. At one point, I try grabbing handfuls of paper off the floor and flinging them overhead, shaking my feet so my claws clatter, and squeaking ecstatically. This is a keeper; even Pitney is chortling. I've been a little hard on him; he's not such a bad guy. Then we do the shot with the giant copier. The doors of the copier are open, and they've got it rigged to spew out shredded paper from the side. I'm supposed to nose around, lift the various levers and pull out drawers. I throw in the ear scratch bit, and it gets a good laugh from Pitney. Then I scrabble over to the side of the copier where the paper is coming out and start stuffing paper into my mouth. It's an inspired bit, and the crew is laughing. As I'm doing this, I hear a voice on my right. "A rat's not gonna eat the paper. He should just sniff it." I twist around and grab a peek—it's one of the agency goons, Ben Some-body. Everybody wants to direct.

I raise my eyebrows, à la Jack Benny, and hold up my rodent paws in appeal to my audience. This is a bad move, and I know better. I'm just the hired rat. You don't bite the hand that feeds you.

Pitney is nodding earnestly, the weenie, doing his best to pacify the suits. "Good point, yes. So, Dan, let's try that. Just sniffing the paper as it comes out." I sniff.

By the time they're done with me, I'm starving, but the catering table has been cleaned out—lots of crumb-dusted trays, wadded napkins, and used paper plates with half-eaten muffins, crusts of quiche, and melon rinds—and another three hours before lunch. I grab a couple of glazed donuts and a cup of sour coffee, and Jodi takes me to my dressing room. Halfway there, we pass a guy coming the other way. He looks like something you might see at a sinister theme park: an enormous white rat in standard issue business attire—pale blue dress shirt, rep tie, chalk-striped trousers—but minus the paws, which I've left on the set. There's a large furry headpiece with pink ears and eyes, a pointed snout maybe two feet long and with stiff plastic whiskers. Human eyes peer out through wire mesh in the mouth. A bubble of anxiety loosens in my bowels. As we pass, I take note of the long, rubbery tail emerging from the seat of his trousers.

"That's the stand-in," Jodi informs me. "I got assaulted at a club," she adds, making conversation. The remark strikes me as a bizarre segue until I remember that, in theory, we are fellow crime victims.

"These guys come up behind me and one of them, he, like, smashes me on the head with a beer bottle. For no reason. I was just standing there. I had to have six stitches." As she's talking, I realize that what I had taken for a speech impediment is actually a tiny silver barbell implanted in her tongue. I am attracted and repelled in about equal measure.

"Is that what happened to you?" she asks.

"What?" I snap back into the present moment.

"Were you, like, an innocent bystander?"

"No, I guess I provoked this one."

We have arrived at my dressing room. She points me inside and tells me that Sheila will help me with the costume when they're ready. I thank her, but she hangs in the doorway expectantly.

"So, did you try to fight them for your wallet?" She brushes a wisp of invisible hair out of her face and squirms against the door.

"No. I didn't have my wallet with me. I was just out walking my dog." For some reason, it seems important to stay on the technical side of the truth.

Her expression brightens with childlike glee. "Oohhh," she coos. "You have a dog?"

What the hell, I go ahead and invite Jodi into my dressing room. I offer her one of my donuts, which she declines with a wrinkled nose.

Girls are one of the perks of being an actor. You might think that you'd have to be a handsome leading man to get the women, but I am proof positive that this is not the case. Even a thirty-seven-year-old schmoe playing a lab rat in a commercial and with one eye resembling a rotting onion can, in fact, attract women. Not grown women perhaps, but it's not a quibble to give the average guy pause. Not this one anyway. It even crosses my mind that maybe I could get along in the world without Robin after all, armed as I am with a dog and a SAG card.

Jodi and I compare notes on urban crime and I relate, immodestly, my recent encounter with the burglar in my apartment. She is rapt as I recount his demand that I get down on the floor, my refusal, his threatening me with the paring knife. "And the funny thing is," I tell her, "I was calm the whole time. Calm is not my usual style," I admit, "but I was talking to this guy like I was his shrink."

A stickler for the truth, I don't neglect to include Robin in the story, but the mention of a wife doesn't cause any visible wrinkle in Jodi's attention. This means that either I have misjudged her interest or she is one of those young women for whom a wife is not regarded as the slightest impediment. Either way, it dampens my enthusiasm. I cannot pretend, not even long enough for a protracted flirtation, that I am not married.

"I have a couple of calls to make," I tell her. "Is there a phone somewhere I can use?"

"There's a pay phone back the way we came."

"Thanks, Jodi. I'll see you later." I wait for her to exit, and then follow her down the hall at a safe distance.

When I dial the number in Maine, I fully expect to get the answering machine—this will be my fourth message in three days, not counting hang-ups—and I'm trying to decide how much to say, specifically whether I should mention my black eye, which would then involve explaining how I came to attack a complete stranger on the street last night, when I hear Robin's voice. I'm startled into silence until she says hello again, this time phrased as a suspicious question.

"It's me."

"Dan." She says my name in a pitch that suggests someone else is in the room with her. "I tried to call you."

"I know. I'm sorry. I was out with Stuart and it got late, and then when I tried to call you yesterday, you were gone."

"How's Stuart?" Still the neutral conversational mode.

"He's fine, I guess. He's working on one of those books, some Eastern mystic's guide to striking it rich in the stock market, so every time he opens his mouth, he sounds like a late-night FM disc jockey. But other than that, he's good."

I translate the length and weight of her silence like Morse code: whoever was there has cleared out, and she doesn't have to be polite anymore.

"I got the commercial," I tell her. "Actually, that's where I'm calling from. I'm on a break now."

"That's good, right?" I don't know whether she means that it's good I'm on a break or good that I booked the commercial, but her inflection indicates that she is impatient with this chitchat. If I called simply to tell her I booked this stupid commercial, she's got better things to do. My sleep-deprived brain is slogging along at a maddeningly slow pace, and I can't devise what to say next. How to . . .

"So, what's going on, Robin?" I blurt. "Are you going to leave me?"

There is another exquisitely full silence, and I know without a doubt that she has been considering this very question, that she is considering it still, as we speak. Telepathy is hardly the occult talent it's made out to be; spend eleven years with another person, each of you curbing your own will and trying to bend the other's, trying, that is, to twine in the same general direction, and you find that words become not unnecessary but supplemental.

"I don't know. It's not that I want to. But . . ." She stops and we both mentally review all the good reasons she has to leave.

"I don't want you to," I say.

"I know."

And there we are. There is another painful silence that I don't know how to fill. The thing I want to say—the world would be empty without you—I can't seem to say, although it's true. One of the comforts of marriage has been the dailiness that doesn't require or even allow poetic passion. And so I suppose our vocabulary has become stunted by familiarity. Often, I will tell her I love her in the perfunctory way of ending phone calls or saying good night. I'll listen with one ear cocked to the game while she tells me the events of her day. We bump companionably along, adjusting without thinking if something chafes. Oh, now and again I'll happen to glance at her standing in front of the bathroom mirror in one of my old T-shirts, and my breath will catch unexpectedly. Or she'll casually disclose some facet of herself that she's just never happened to mention—she can walk on the backs of her toes, she was state champ in women's archery, she wants to go to the Galápagos Islands before she dies—and I'll have a fleeting rush of admiration for what an amazing, original woman she is. But for long stretches I am as unaware of Robin as of my own breath. Only now that I am jerked up short by the possibility of loss, when I see that love, too, is mortal and fragile, only now do I fully realize what I stand to lose here.

"Is it living in New York?" I ask. "I mean, is that what we're talking about?" I'm not at all sure that I can quit the city, but if that's what's required, I want to know.

"I don't want to do this on the phone, Dan. Let's wait until I get home."

Long after we have said good-bye, I am still holding the receiver and staring into some vague middle distance. The phone squawks for a while, then eventually falls silent. When I bring the receiver back to my ear, I hear the sound of the sea.

I pass a blank hour before the wardrobe person, Sheila, arrives with the costume and supervises my dressing. I'm guessing she must have small children at home. She tells me to strip to my shorts, and while I do, she watches with total disinterest. Then she hands me one item of the costume at a time, first the undershirt, then the furry white knee-high socks, then the crisp blue dress shirt, all the while narrating her views on street crime as I dress. She holds up the trousers but then retracts them.

"Do you need to pee first?" she asks.

I assure her I'm fine, but she is unconvinced.

"There's a girdle in here to keep the tail erect. Once we've got you in, you're in for the duration."

She waits while I excuse myself into the adjacent bathroom. I shut the door and then stand at the toilet and urinate, aware as I'm doing so that the sound of my stream is audible in the next room. When I return, Sheila picks up her story where she left off. She picks up the rubber tail, which looks astonishingly like a phallus, except of course that it is roughly three feet long and ends in a point. A fantasy dick, the kind you have in your dreams. It's attached on one end to fabric panels which she wraps and cinches snugly around my waist.

"How about strapping this on the front?" I smirk.

"Don't you wish." Sheila smiles wearily and shakes her head. Boys, the mother of unruly boys. Then she helps me into Lab Rat's trousers, threading the tail through a hole in the seat and tucking my shirt in. She allows me to zip on my own.

We strap on my paws, first the feet, then the hands. Finally, Lab Rat's head. Sheila climbs onto a chair and lifts the huge head from the dressing table where it has been staring at me with beady, blank malevolence for the past twenty minutes. A tie dangles loosely from its neck. She hoists the monster above my own head, but before she can lower it, I grab her wrists, surprising us both. A chilly sweat has popped out of my pores.

"Could we wait on the head?"

Her eyebrows lift.

"Just until we get onto the set?"

"Suit yourself."

Half-man, half-rat, I follow Sheila down the hallway. I have a sudden, powerful empathy for the death-row prisoner being led to his execution. The fact that my dread makes no sense does nothing to lessen its insistence, and by the time we get to the soundstage, my heart is fairly skittering inside my ribs. There are several more people milling around than were here earlier, and the set is throbbing with hot light. I'm feeling a bit woozy and have to close my eyes for a moment against the light and noise, the buzz of voices. Under the drumbeat of my heart, I can hear Pitney's voice issuing instructions to the cameraman, and another voice saying we need to get those cables taped down before someone breaks his neck.

"Is he okay?"

"I dunno."

"Dan?" I open my eyes and Pitney is standing directly in front of me, silhouetted darkly against the glare. "Ready to rock and roll?" he asks. Sheila is behind him, and she's got one arm wrapped around Lab Rat's snout, the other grasping its open neck. I can't speak, but I attempt a smile and a nod. Sheila, my executioner, holds out the empty head. When I peer inside, there is nothing but blackness and, in the distance, two pinpricks of light, the eyeholes. They are impossibly far away, and I realize with a heart-jolting certainty that there's no way I can get enough air in my lungs to make it that far. I take a shallow gulp, though, and I try. I shut my eyes, and I swallow another breath and then another and then, God help me, I pull the head down over my own, but just as I feared, I'm not going to make it. Waves of panic crest over me, my air is running out, and I can't find the eyeholes. When I try to extricate myself, one of my damn claws gets hung up on something. I am on the verge of passing out before I finally yank myself free.

"You okay there?" Pitney asks.

I find enough breath to whisper the word "fine." This is so clearly a lie, I have to amend it. "Just give me a minute," I wheeze. "I'm a little dizzy is all." I shrug my shoulders as though to suggest I'm just as mystified as he is.

Teeka swims into view. Her head is shaking slightly, a little tremor of disgust. "Are you claustrophobic, Dan?" She might as well be asking me if I have gonorrhea. I study the question carefully. Claustrophobia? No, I wouldn't call it that, exactly. Perhaps some discomfort in dark, enclosed spaces. I try to avoid being trapped in dark and enclosed spaces, how's that?

I was five or six years old, and my brother, Ricky, and I were playing magician. Ricky tied our mother's red skirt around his neck, drew a mustache on his upper lip with what turned out to be an indelible laundry marker, and christened himself the Truly Amazing Ricardo. Being the younger sibling, I was assigned the role of magician's assistant, the one who picked a playing card out of the deck (a card, any card, not that one) and stood against the wall with a handkerchief tied around my eyes while he threw silverware at me. Anything to be in the show. Then Ricky got the brilliant idea to lock me in the hope chest at the foot of our parents' bed. This was thirty years ago, but I can still vividly recall the suffocating blackness of my blanket-lined coffin, the sharp smell of mothballs, the muffled voice of my brother explaining to our imaginary audience that he had nothing up his sleeves. And then his voice was drowned out by screams. Mine, as it turned out.

Someone has found a chair, but I can't sit down, not with my damn tail, so they instruct me to bend over at the waist. I stare down at the floor and see paws where my feet should be, paws at the center of a circle of human feet. "Take slow, deep breaths," a voice is saying. I overhear another voice, farther away. "What's the problem?" and then "You gotta be kidding me."

I try again, valiantly, but each time I descend into the interior of Lab Rat's head, I am engulfed by fresh panic, a panic exacerbated now by the fear that my career is crashing before my eyes. When I reemerge, gasping and blinking away my blindness, I am confronted by a gallery of stone faces, the veneer of patience worn thin. I try again. It's no use. Even if I could stay inside the head for a few minutes, there is no way I could simultaneously remember to move and breathe, much less climb the exercise wheel. While this is not a demanding role, it does require motor skills.

By now, the news has spread to everyone on the set: the actor is freaking out and can't get his head inside the rat costume. An impromptu powwow is called a few feet away. Because I am the subject of discussion, they are careful to lower their voices, so I can't make out most of what is being said. But I can guess. I hear Pitney issue orders to find the stand-in, and there is more murmured discussion, punctured by a crackle of laughter before the group breaks up. Preparations are underway to move forward without me.

My panic has begun to subside, and I'm pretty certain I could stand up without getting woozy. But I stay bent over all the same. I can't bring myself to face anyone. Besides, it would be unseemly to recover so readily. Indeed, I'm guessing it will be viewed by some as bad taste on my part not to expire right on the spot. I would happily accommodate them if I could. If this is not the most humiliating hour in my life, it's right up there.

Sheila appears again at my side, and as though she is talking me off a ledge, she explains that they'll need to get me out of the costume. It's all right, she says, no need to move just yet. She's brought my own clothes from the dressing room. First the paws, she says. When I lift my head, I see my street clothes in a heap on the chair. She means, I realize, to strip me right here.

"I can walk to the dressing room," I say. I intend my tone to convey steadiness, but it must sound angry to Sheila because she steels her gaze and looks right through me.

"They need the costume."

And sure enough, the stand-in, who has been recruited to take my place, is poised just on the other side of the set, behind the giant pellet dispenser. He is talking with Pitney and nodding intently.

I pick up my clothes and walk away, not as far as the dressing room but far enough to get out of the circle of broiling lights and into the relative anonymity behind the cameras. Sheila strips me of Lab Rat's costume, piece by piece, and returns me to my human state. She gathers up the costume, and I am alone. I watch at a distance as she suits up the stand-in. He snugs on that rat's head as though it were a stylish hat and hops up onto the wheel, ready to work. Pitney instructs him to lie back on the wheel and bicycle his legs, and the stand-in obliges, looking more robotic than frantic. Still, let's be frank, there's not much acting required here. He can put on the suit and follow instructions, and in the end, that's what counts.

I'm at a loss what to do now. I wait for a while, vacillating between the hope that someone will appear and direct me and the hope that, mercifully, I have been forgotten. Finally, I search out Teeka, moving around the edges of the soundstage from one clump of people to the next. As I pass, there is a perceptible ripple of awareness, but they each do their best to pretend I don't exist. Only Sheila actually makes eye contact, and she lets me know with a look that, as much as she would like to sympathize, I have brought this on myself. Now, it goes without saying that there are a lot of people here who would just as soon I'd never shown up this morning. After all, they have to rehearse the new guy, and this little fiasco is going to set back the schedule a couple of hours. By the same token, though, there should also be at least a few union people on this set who would have a generous thought for me, as I will no doubt be responsible for some overtime, possibly even golden time. If so, they keep it to themselves. I am being shunned, as surely as if I had a scarlet *A* on my breast for Actor.

When I find her, Teeka is painstakingly professional. She tells me in clipped tones that she's put a call in to my union rep. She's never had to deal with this situation before, so she's not sure what the procedure is. As she understands it, if I want to get paid the session rate, I may have to stay on call. In any case, I'll at least have to wait until she hears back. If I want to wait in the dressing room, that's fine. Everything in her demeanor suggests that I have pulled a fast one, that I may have conned the rest of them, but she for one is not buying.

It is only now that I remember I have an agent. This is what he gets paid for. I beg some change off Sheila and retreat down the hall to the pay phone.

"Good afternoon—Shepard, Pape, and Associates."

I recognize the voice of one of the associates. No one is a receptionist anymore; they are all associate agents. So theoretically this guy, Patrick, represents me, but neither he nor I see it quite that way.

I ask to speak to Zak, and he deflects me.

"He's on another line. Can I take a message and have him ring you back?"

"No, I need to talk to him."

Patrick repeats woodenly, "He's on another line."

"No shit. I need to talk to him now." I speak slowly, in case he's an idiot. "Not later. Now."

Patrick has no easy reply for this. I have violated the carefully honed rules of his universe: actors with status give orders; actors without status plead and grovel. I hear a click, and for a split second, I figure he's hung up on me, but then the tinny strains of salsa pipe through the phone.

If I were going to start worrying about my career at this late date, I could mull over the fact that I have just alienated one of the people whose job it is to make sure my résumés get submitted to the casting people, a person who will probably never again let me speak to my agent.

"Dan." Zak's mouth is full and I hear him chewing something, chew, chew, swallow. "So what's this big emergency?"

"Zak, I'm sorry to bother you." Now that I've got him on the phone, I'm not sure where to go from here.

"Patrick tells me you ripped him a new asshole."

"Tell him I'm sorry."

"Yeah, yeah. Between you and me." He chuckles. "Ah, never mind."

"It's this commercial thing."

Zak takes another bite. "What's that? Oh, yeah, the Dobbins national. Aren't you shooting that today?"

"Zak, I fucked up."

"What do you mean you fucked up?" I now have his complete attention.

"There's a head. The costume has a big headpiece, and I couldn't wear it."

"I'm not following you."

"I couldn't put the head on. I get claustrophobic. No one ever said anything about a big head, or I would have told them."

There is a pause while Zak attempts to make sense of this.

"So you're at the studios, yes? And what are they doing?"

"They're rehearsing the stand-in."

"And no one ever mentioned this headpiece to you? Not during one of the auditions, maybe?"

"No. I mean maybe I should have assumed."

Zak jumps in. "Fuck that. That's not your job. That's their job." I can hear him working out his strategy. "Someone should have informed us if the costume required special skills."

I could weep with gratitude.

"Forget about it. Go home. Make sure you sign the pa-perwork."

"I'm sorry, Zak."

"What are you apologizing to me for? Go home, get drunk, whatever. There'll be other jobs."

Yes. Other jobs. Of course. A tiny bright light winks in the blackness, like the eyeholes in the rat's head, far away but bright. This time, though, I may make it. I take a deep breath.

"Speaking of which," I say, "you haven't heard anything from Tribeca yet, have you? I know it's early, but I had a re-ally good feeling about that one."

Zak clears his throat. "They went with someone else, Dan."

There is a fly on the wall, right at eye level. I could move to the desert like Robin wants. To hell with these people. This life. My chest feels heavy like it's covered with a lead X-ray apron.

"But Helen said they loved you, that you read like a house afire. They just decided to go a different way. You know Kyle McCann? He's one of ours. Maybe you met him at the Christmas party."

"I gotta go."

"Okay, kiddo. Sign the papers."

It's three in the morning and I'm driving up I–95, headed to Maine. Just past Boston, the jazz station I've been listening to dims and sputters out. A little farther north, Puck, too, grows quiet, finally exhausted after hours of lurching around the interior of Stuart's car, whining and stress-shedding on the immaculate upholstery. He is asleep now on the seat beside me, dreaming who knows what, his paws lightly beating the air. There is only the occasional car. The night is quiet and dark and empty. Living without a car for the past fourteen years, I had forgotten how intoxicating it is to drive alone at night. Cocooned in Stuart's snug little Honda, I might go anywhere. The world becomes a series of possible destinations, the road signs lit up like invitations. And behind me, New York recedes like a weirdly distorted dream, a dream peopled with outsized rats' heads and boys with baggy pants and enormous running shoes, boys who are running from me. I need to catch up, to explain something, but no matter how hard I push myself, I don't seem to be any closer. I am running and running, and then suddenly I am on a wheel and my feet have become paws and I am running, still running. And Judy Garland is dancing, her knees and elbows pumping, her smile game, her eyes wide with fear.

That was hours ago, years ago, a lifetime ago. If it weren't for the hollow ache in my gut, I could almost pretend that none of it had ever happened.

I roll down the window, just in case I'm sleepier than I think. The air is cool and smells like seawater. I haven't yet figured out what I'll say to Robin. She doesn't even know I'm coming. I should probably pull over and sleep, but I'm afraid that if I did, when I woke up I wouldn't have the courage to do whatever it is I'm about to do. A little sleep might put this all in the flat, reasonable perspective of daylight.

I remember the first night I went on stage in New York. I didn't come on until near the end of the first act, but I was too antsy to wait in the empty dressing room, so I came upstairs early. I stood in the dusty dark behind the back set wall and listened to the spill of familiar lines, mixed now with the laughter of an audience, a stray titter, a cough. The play was zipping along, and as my entrance drew closer, I started nervously running my lines in my head. A few lines in, I blanked. Suddenly, I couldn't remember what came next. Nothing, not what Rob said, not what I said, not a single line of the play from that point forward. Nothing but sheer blank terror. The bottom fell out of my stomach. I had a fleeting notion that I could run downstairs and grab the script off my makeup table, check the lines, find my place. But on stage, they were maybe six lines from my cue. Five. Four. I moved stolidly toward the stage right wing, to the edge of the light, and before I could think any further, there was my cue. I took a deep breath and walked into the blinding light, like stepping out of a plane and into the sky, trusting the chute will open.

Of course, it did. No problem. Once on stage, I was home. I knew what to do as if I'd been doing it all my life. The lines appeared as they were needed, as though I had just thought of them. And it was exhilarating, living in that moment, knowing only peripherally what might come next.

The moon, sweeping in and out of clouds, follows at a distance. The engine hums, the dog snores, pavement unrolls beneath the headlights. If some miracle were to occur and I was able to sleep again, this is what I would miss.

Insights,
Interviews
& More . . .

Meet Debra Dean

David Hiller

About the author

> **❝ I had no model for writing books as something that people still did. I think subconsciously I figured you needed three names or at the very least a British accent. ❞**

DEBRA DEAN was born and raised in Seattle, Washington. The daughter of a builder and a homemaker and artist, she was a bookworm but never imagined becoming a writer. "Growing up, I read Louisa May Alcott and Laura Ingalls Wilder, Jane Austen and the Brontës," she said. "Until I left college, I rarely read anyone who hadn't been dead for at least fifty years, so I had no model for writing books as something that people still did. I think subconsciously I figured you needed three names or at the very least a British accent."

At Whitman College, Dean double-majored in English and drama: "If you can imagine anyone being this naïve, I figured if the acting thing didn't work out, I'd have the English major to fall back on." After college, she moved to New York and spent two years at the Neighborhood Playhouse,

2

a professional actors' training program. She worked in New York and regional theater for nearly a decade, and met her future husband when they were cast as brother and sister in A. R. Gurney's play *The Dining Room*. "If I'd had a more successful career as an actor, I'd probably still be doing it because I loved acting," she said. "I understudied in a couple of long-running plays, so I was able to keep my union health insurance, but the business is pretty dreadful. When I started thinking about getting out, I had no idea what else I might do. What I eventually came up with was writing, which in many ways was a comically ill-advised choice, given that the pitfalls of writing as a career are nearly identical to acting. One key difference, though, is that you don't have to be hired before you can write. Another big advantage is that you don't need to get facelifts or even be presentable: most days, I can wear my ratty old jeans and T-shirts and not bother with the hair and makeup."

In 1990, Dean moved back to the Northwest and got her MFA at the University of Oregon. She started teaching writing and publishing her short stories in literary journals. *The Madonnas of Leningrad*, her first novel, was published in 2006. It was a *New York Times* Editors' Choice and a finalist for the Quill Award and the Guardian First Book Award (UK).

"In retrospect," she said, "I'm very grateful for my circuitous journey, that I wasn't some wunderkind. I like to think I have more compassion now and a perspective that I didn't have when I was younger." ⌒

> " In retrospect, I'm very grateful for my circuitous journey, that I wasn't some wunderkind. "

A Conversation with Debra Dean

You wrote these stories in the 1990s. Describe your life during that time. Were you acting much?

No, I made a clean break from acting when I left New York in 1990—burned my union cards and cut off my hair. Very dramatic. When I was writing these stories, I was living in Eugene, Oregon, and then Seattle, teaching writing and literature.

Did your schedule prevent novelistic undertakings?

For years I had a very heavy teaching load, and it probably didn't help. Lots of writers teach and write simultaneously, but it's a challenge to do both well. Especially with a novel, which requires so much psychic space. You have only so much time, and you choose whether your writing or students come first. Invariably, I chose my students, in part because theirs were the more insistent voices. If I found a little breathing space, I'd work on a short story. William Carlos Williams used to write poems on prescription pads between patients, and his poems are prescription-pad length. My stories are a little longer, but the principle is the same.

That said, I also think the schedule was a bit of a dodge. The truth is, I was terrified by the sheer volume of a novel because I'm such a painstakingly slow, line-by-line writer. Of course, *The Madonnas of Leningrad* is short as novels go.

How did you happen to start writing short stories?

I needed a creative vent when I wasn't acting, and the two—acting and fiction writing—are very similar. You're basically pretending your way into an imagined life. At the time, I thought I was making an unusual career transition, but I've since met any number of actors-turned-writers.

> 66 William Carlos Williams used to write poems on prescription pads between patients, and his poems are prescription-pad length. My stories are a little longer, but the principle is the same. 99

The 1990s—what did you write with back then, a stylus or a quill?

(Laughs) I bought my first computer when I started grad school in 1990. It ran DOS Word Perfect and used those big floppy disks. Prior to that, I had written in loose-leaf notebooks with a fountain pen. I don't know that I could go back to writing by hand, but I think about it sometimes because the ease of deleting and revising as I write is such an irresistible temptation.

Did you associate much with other writers?

Well, I am a product of an MFA program, but after school, I pretty much worked in solitude. I have writer friends, but we don't talk much about writing, and I've generally avoided more structured writing groups. I have nothing against them, mind you, and I do think it's good to have the emotional support, especially when you're starting out, the reassurance from others that you're not completely insane. But writers are loners. That's the nature of it.

Whom did you regard as your audience—friends? family?

I wrote for a largely imaginary audience back then—myself as a reader multiplied several times over. A few others read my stories: my husband always reads everything first because he's a wonderful editor by nature, and he gets what I'm trying to do. When I was still in school, teachers and fellow writers were my audience. Later, editors of literary journals and eventually the devoted little cadre of people who read those journals. But I didn't really write with any of them in mind. My sense of an audience was more abstract.

It continues to startle me to have flesh-and-blood readers who get in touch with me or meet me at readings. They've frequently had ▶

> **My husband always reads everything first because he's a wonderful editor by nature, and he gets what I'm trying to do.**

A Conversation with Debra Dean *(continued)*

remarkable insights and observations, and I've learned a lot about what I've written by listening to them. But the trick is to leave those readers outside the door when you go back into the writing room. It's deadly when you start anticipating readers' responses.

Of the stories collected in this volume, which do you care for most?

Isn't that like asking a mother which child is her favorite? Even if you have an answer, you probably shouldn't admit it. I'm afraid I'm hopelessly subjective about these stories, and I like different things about each one.

Which gave you the most trouble?

The stories that gave me the most trouble aren't published. I don't mind a reasonable amount of trouble, but at a certain point, if the story isn't coming together, I think you have to listen to that—there's probably a good reason.

Are you an obsessive plotter of stories, or do you just sit down and have at it?

I envy those writers who plot and storyboard—I secretly imagine that it must be easier for them because they know where they're headed. But when I've tried it, what I come up with is a little flat and formulaic. I'm better off just setting out in a general direction and allowing myself to be surprised. It's not good from a time-management point of view—I take a lot of detours—but it allows me the possibility of stumbling onto something better than I'd planned.

❝ I'm a hopeless tinkerer. ❞

How do you know when a story is finished?

It's finished when it's ripped out of my hands. I'm a hopeless tinkerer.

In a 2006 interview with NPR, you had this to say about your novel The Madonnas of Leningrad: *"I initially thought that I was going to write a short story about my grandmother who was in the early stages of Alzheimer's, and I was just fascinated by her experience with memory. She was losing her short-term memory and forgetting words and repeating stories, but at the same time, paradoxically, her long-term memory was becoming much more intense for her, and she was telling stories that I had never heard before." How did this short story snowball into a novel?*

I started what I thought was going to be a short story set during the siege of Leningrad. I started writing another story having to do with my grandmother and her experience of Alzheimer's, and the two stories started to weave together. I loved the story, but it became apparent that the scope of it was too large to be contained in the short form. I couldn't imagine when I was going to write a novel, so come September, I put it away and started my classes again.

Meanwhile, I had gotten an agent for this collection, which was a minor miracle because agenting short stories is pro bono work, and most agents understandably hold out for novels, but to my eternal gratitude, Marly has a wide streak of idealism. At some point, she and I were going through my stories to put together the collection, and I sent her my unfinished Leningrad piece. I told her that it was probably supposed to be a novel, but perhaps I could still bludgeon it back into a short story to include in the collection. She came back to me with this: "I know you don't want to write a novel, but you need to write this one. I'm going to hold the short story collection until you're done and market them together." My car was falling apart, and I had really hoped she would sell the stories for enough money to buy a slightly newer ▶

clunker, so initially I was disappointed, but it was the push I needed.

Were you unnerved to find yourself tackling a novel?

I backed into it over such a long period. By the time I figured out that what I had been writing was a novel, and not a short story or a novella, some of the fear was replaced by excitement. And then I just wrote it in manageable little pieces, like patches of a quilt.

How has your life changed since the nineties? And how has this affected the quantity and quality of your writing?

For starters—this is a little silly—but it's a lot easier for me to say out loud that I'm a writer when I can produce physical evidence in the form of a book. HarperCollins also gave me enough money to take a couple of years off from teaching. I envisioned myself holing up and just writing, but the reality turned out to be quite different. *The Madonnas of Leningrad* got a lot of attention, which was incredibly fortunate, but with that comes the daily minutiae of publicity and travel. I really enjoy all that, but it's a very different energy from the musing solitude of writing.

I've since started another novel that demands a lot of research. And I've returned to teaching, quite happily. I've come to realize that one is always juggling the writing with other things. That's why writers have fantasy camps—Yaddo and such places where you go for a few weeks and it's all about the writing—but most of us can't really live that way for very long.

Have you written any short stories lately?

No. I have a couple ideas on the back burner, but I don't want to be distracted from the novel.

> 66 By the time I figured out that what I had been writing was a novel, and not a short story or a novella, some of the fear was replaced by excitement. And then I just wrote it in manageable little pieces, like patches of a quilt. 99

Which short story writers engage you most?

(Laughs) This always feels like an exam question.
Or like I'm opening my underwear drawer for
inspection. Well, let's see what's in there—I'm
looking at my bookshelves for help because I
only keep what I love. Here's Andrea Barrett's
collection, *Ship Fever*. And *Tabloid Dreams* by
Robert Olen Butler. Farther down, in the *C*s,
some of the usual suspects: Chekhov, of course,
and Raymond Carver and John Cheever. I won't
bore you with the whole alphabet, but I can't leave
out Grace Paley. Oh, and Jane Smiley's *The Age of
Grief*. They make the cut every time I move.

What are you reading now?

Mostly research material and student stories.
But I just finished Patricia Hampl's new memoir,
The Florist's Daughter. I'm humbled by her
writing; it's really beautiful and incisive. And
every night I've been turning in with a few short
chapters of Tolstoy's memoir, *Childhood, Boyhood,
Youth.* ❧

More Confessions: The Stories Behind the Book

I AM ABOUT to move again and am facing with dread the prospect of weeding out the bulk of stuff that I cannot take with me. Like Elaine in my story "Another Little Piece," I am a compulsive archivist. It pains me to throw out anything—a thirty-year-old souvenir T-shirt from a rafting trip through the Grand Canyon, a paper plate covered in ribbons that I carried at my wedding rehearsal in place of a bouquet, the puppy collar belonging to a long-dead spaniel—there is no memento that doesn't call up a memory or that might not be useful again. Even while I recognize the spiritual wisdom in the Buddhist's non-attachment to material things, I am indiscriminately smitten with it all. What I imagine I will do with a set of oval flan dishes or the gray felt hat trimmed in ostrich feathers baffles even me, but someday they may come in handy.

I suspect this habit of thinking is shared by other writers of short stories. Our craft invites us to keep sorting through the heaped-up past, plucking out small moments, and holding them up to see how they catch the light. I can look over these stories in *Confessions of a Falling Woman* and find scraps from my own life over two decades. Like the protagonist in "What the Left Hand Is Saying," I was once a young actress who lived in a fifth-floor walk-up in New York (just a few blocks from the offices of HarperCollins), and I had a roommate who was a puppeteer. I moved to Brooklyn, and that lovely apartment on Prospect Park later became the setting for "Dan in the Gray Flannel Rat Suit." There actually was a burglar who broke in though the kitchen window, held my husband at knifepoint, and then thought better of it and left. My husband, Cliff, also an actor, was once hired to spend a day dressed in a rodent costume for a video game.

> 66 Like Elaine in my story 'Another Little Piece,' I am a compulsive archivist. It pains me to throw out anything. 99

I hoard my own past, but I also save shiny bits of overheard conversation and the mental refuse that other people have thrown away. I met a woman who told me that she and her siblings referred to their mother as the Queen Mother. I know nothing else about the woman or her mother, but her passing remark was the seed of "The Queen Mother," a story set (for reasons even I cannot explain) in Baton Rouge, where I spent one uneventful night on a six-month tour of a play. My only memory of Baton Rouge is the Howard Johnson's, but that tour also took me to Sarasota, Florida, and the pelicans and purple theater in that town made it into "Romance Manual." My former shrink, who bears some passing resemblance to the Buddhist shrink in "The Bodhisattva," came back from Bangkok and described to me the difficulty of building a psychiatric practice in a culture that rejects notions of guilt. The green silk picture he brought back of Hanuman, the monkey general, is still here somewhere. A friend who later died from a brain tumor told me that one of the symptoms of the tumor was smelling burning rubber. Though there is nothing else belonging to Fred in the story "Confessions of a Falling Woman," when I read it, I think of him.

However, more than any biographical details of character or setting or plot, what is most true about these stories is universal. There is a haunting poem by Elizabeth Bishop that begins "The art of losing isn't hard to master." She goes on to list the inevitable losses in one's life, beginning with the innocuous—mittens and keys and so on—and escalating to the loss of places one has lived and people one has loved. For me it was the loss of memory brought on by disease (Alzheimer's) that became the inspiration for my first novel. Bishop spurs herself to the end with the injunction "Write it!" These stories work that same ground, exploring what it means to move forward, always leaving something precious behind.

I went to the graduation last night of a ▶

> " I met a woman who told me that she and her siblings referred to their mother as the Queen Mother. I know nothing else about the woman or her mother, but her passing remark was the seed of 'The Queen Mother.' "

More Confessions *(continued)*

goddaughter whose life Cliff and I have been
privileged to share for nearly eighteen years.
She is off to college in Ohio, we are off to
Miami, and her parents are also moving to
another state, so this may well have been the
last of many evenings spent talking and laughing
around a table together. A life rich with friends
and family and interesting work is also, perforce,
a life filled with losses. Even the most comic
moments are recalled with a catch in the throat.
If you are a writer, you save it all. ⤳

The Madonnas of
Leningrad: An Excerpt

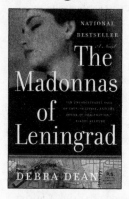

In the following excerpt from The Madonnas of
Leningrad, *the ravages of age are eroding Marina's
grip on the everyday. An elderly Russian woman
now living in America, she cannot hold on to fresh
memories—the details of her grown children's lives,
the approaching wedding of her grandchild—yet
her distant past is miraculously preserved in her
mind's eye.*

*Vivid images of her youth in war-torn Leningrad
arise unbidden, carrying her back to the terrible fall
of 1941, when she was a tour guide at the Hermitage
Museum and the German army's approach signaled
the beginning of what would be a long, torturous
siege on the city. As the people braved starvation,
bitter cold, and a relentless German onslaught,
Marina joined other staff members in removing
the museum's priceless masterpieces for safekeeping,
leaving the frames hanging empty on the walls to
symbolize the artworks' eventual return. As the
Luftwaffe's bombs pounded the proud, stricken
city, Marina built a personal Hermitage in her
mind—a refuge that would stay buried deep
within her, until she needed it once more. . . .*

This way, please. We are standing in the Spanish
Skylight Hall. The three skylight halls were ▶

The Madonnas of Leningrad:
An Excerpt *(continued)*

designed to display the largest canvases in the collection. Look up. The huge vault and frieze are like a wedding cake, with molded and gilt arabesques. Light streams down on parquet floors the color of wheat, and the walls are painted a rich red in imitation of the original cloth covering. Each of the skylight halls is decorated with exquisite vases, standing candelabra, and tabletops made of semiprecious stones in the Russian mosaic technique.

Over here, to our left, is a table with a heavy white cloth. Three Spanish peasants are eating lunch. The fellow in the center is raising the decanter of wine and offering us a drink. Clearly, they are enjoying themselves. Their luncheon is light—a dish of sardines, a pomegranate, and a loaf of bread—but it is more than enough. A whole loaf of bread, and white bread at that, not the blockade bread that is mostly wood shavings.

The other residents of the museum are allotted only three small chunks of bread each day. Bread the size and color of pebbles. And sometimes frozen potatoes, potatoes dug from a garden at the edge of the city. Before the siege, Director Orbeli ordered great quantities of linseed oil to repaint the walls of the museum. We fry bits of potato in the linseed oil. Later, when the potatoes and oil are gone, we make a jelly out of the glue used to bind frames and eat that.

The man on the right, giving us a thumbs-up, is probably the artist. Diego Rodríguez de Silva y Velázquez. This is from his early Seville period, a type of painting called *bodegones*, "scenes in taverns."

It is as though she has been transported into a two-dimensional world, a book perhaps, and she exists only on this page. When the page turns, whatever was on the previous page disappears from her view.

Marina finds herself standing in front of the kitchen sink, holding a saucepan of water. But she

> 66 Before the siege, Director Orbeli ordered great quantities of linseed oil to repaint the walls of the museum. We fry bits of potato in the linseed oil. 99

has no idea why. Is she rinsing the pan? Or has she just finished filling it up? It is a puzzle. Sometimes it requires all her wits to piece together the world with the fragments she is given: an open can of Folgers, a carton of eggs on the counter, the faint scent of toast. Breakfast. Has she eaten? She cannot recall. Well, does she feel hungry or full? Hungry, she decides. And here is the miracle of five white eggs nested in a foam carton. She can almost taste the satiny yellow of the yolks on her tongue. Go ahead, she tells herself, eat.

When her husband, Dmitri, comes into the kitchen carrying the dirty breakfast dishes, she is poaching more eggs.

"What are you doing?" he asks.

She notes the dishes in his hands, the smear of dried yolk in a bowl, the evidence that she has eaten already, perhaps no more than ten minutes ago.

"I'm still hungry." In fact, her hunger has vanished, but she says it nonetheless.

Dmitri sets down the dishes and takes the pan from her hands, sets it down on the counter also. His dry lips graze the back of her neck, and then he steers her out of the kitchen.

"The wedding," he reminds her. "We need to get dressed. Elena called from the hotel and she's on her way."

"Elena is here?"

"She arrived late last night, remember?"

Marina has no recollection of seeing her daughter, and she feels certain she couldn't forget this.

"Where is she?"

"She spent the night at the airport. Her flight was delayed."

"Has she come for the wedding?"

"Yes."

There is a wedding this weekend, but she can't recall the couple who is marrying. Dmitri ▶

> **❝ Marina has no recollection of seeing her daughter, and she feels certain she couldn't forget this. ❞**

says she has met them, and it's not that she doubts him, but . . .

"Now, who is getting married?" she asks.

"Katie, Andrei's girl. To Cooper."

Katie is her granddaughter. But who is Cooper? You'd think she'd remember that name.

"We met him at Christmas," Dmitri says. "And again at Andrei and Naureen's a few weeks ago. He's very tall." He is waiting for some sign of recognition, but there is nothing. "You wore that blue dress with the flowers, and they had salmon for supper," he prompts.

Still nothing. She sees a ghost of despair in his eyes. Sometimes that look is her only hint that something is missing. She begins with the dress. Blue. A blue flowered dress. Bidden, it appears in her mind's eye. She bought it at Penney's.

"It has a pleated collar," she announces triumphantly.

"What's that?" His brow furrows.

"The dress. And branches of lilac flowers." She can call up the exact shade of the fabric. It is the same vivid robin's-egg as the dress worn by the Lady in Blue.

Thomas Gainsborough. *Portrait of the Duchess of Beaufort*. She packed that very painting during the evacuation. She remembers helping to remove it from its gilt frame and then from the stretcher that held it taut.

Whatever is eating her brain consumes only the fresher memories, the unripe moments. Her distant past is preserved, better than preserved. Moments that occurred in Leningrad sixty-some years ago reappear, vivid, plump, and perfumed.

In the Hermitage, they are packing up the picture gallery. It is past midnight but still light enough to see without electricity. It is the end of June 1941. . . . ❧